Blown

AWAY

Blown
AWAY

A Curl Up and Dye Mystery

Nancy Mehl

BARBOUR
PUBLISHING

© 2011 by Nancy Mehl

ISBN 978-1-60260-570-1

For more information about Nancy Mehl, please access the author's Web site at the following Internet address: www.nancymehl.com

Cover design: Faceout Studio, www.faceoutstudio.com

Published by Barbour Publishing, Inc., P.O. Box 719, Uhrichsville, Ohio 44683, www.barbourbooks.com

Our mission is to publish and distribute inspirational products offering exceptional value and biblical encouragement to the masses.

Member of the
Evangelical Christian
Publishers Association

Printed in the United States of America.

DEDICATION

To the members of Wichita Homebound Outreach:
What a blessing it is to count people you admire so tremendously
among your closest friends. Thank you for understanding when
this "writing thing" gets in the way. I love you all so much!

ACKNOWLEDGMENTS

My thanks and appreciation to the following people: To Sandi Megli,
my funeral home expert. Thanks for all your invaluable help. To my
dear friend John Frye, the SPAM king. To Chris Guerrero, hairdresser
extraordinaire! To Tom Monnier, who taught me how to start a fire and
get away with it. (Just kidding!) To meteorologist Mark Bogner from
KSN in Wichita. Thank you for answering my question about tornadoes.
(KSN rocks!) To Faye Spieker and Kim Woodhouse, my dear readers.
To my great editor, Ellen Tarver, for driving me crazy and making me
want to throw my computer out the window. (This is the mark of a really
great editor!) To my wonderful agent, Janet Benrey, who has stood by
my side through this long and sometimes confusing journey. My thanks
to all the great folks at Barbour. And as always, to my family. I love you
guys. Most importantly, to my Father, who has set my feet in a broad
place and given me the desires of my heart.

CHAPTER ⚰ ONE

"I gotta admit, I've seen a lot of weird things in this cemetery," the old groundskeeper said, scratching his head, "but I ain't never seen nothin' like this."

As I gazed down at the dead clown lying faceup at the bottom of a grave dug for someone else, I had to agree. My screams had brought the elderly man running to see what we both now stared at. Harold "Binky" Tuttwiler, dressed in full clown regalia, was definitely deceased, a bloody shovel lying on top of him. Unfortunately, he was taking up space reserved for another clown. Marvin "Bam Bam" Martinez had passed away from an accidental electrocution a few days earlier. He'd been working inside a house that was being renovated as a group home for children with disabilities. Clowns for Christ, an organization both men belonged to, had remodeled several similar homes. This time, though, something had gone terribly wrong. Marvin's funeral was scheduled for this afternoon at two. I had to consider the possibility that Marvin was going to have to wait a bit longer.

"You called the police?" I asked again.

"Yes, miss. I already told you twice. They should be here any minute."

The distant wail of sirens confirmed his statement. I'd also phoned Adam. It was at his request I'd stopped by the cemetery in the first place. Although it was Harold's job to place Marvin's clown hat on his headstone, Adam wanted to make certain he hadn't forgotten. Having a clown funeral without the silly hat was a serious faux pas, I guess. Well, I'd found the hat. Unfortunately, I'd also found Harold.

There was really nothing more to say, so the grounds-keeper and I simply waited as the police and emergency vehicles rushed through the gates. The old man seemed a little unsteady on his feet and sat down on a nearby stone bench. He attempted to pull up his mismatched socks—as if he were trying to tidy himself up for the police. The first emergency vehicle headed our way, but slowly, as if the driver wasn't quite sure where to go. The old man forced himself up and waved his arms to get their attention. For some reason, the idea of an ambulance in a cemetery, searching for a deceased clown, struck me as rather humorous. A little tickle of nervous laughter tried to work its way past my lips. I pushed it back with as much force as I could muster. Standing over a body, giggling maniacally, could get you a trip to jail—or checked into a rubber room. Neither possibility seemed appealing.

The first police car pulled up behind us, and two officers got out. "Are you the folks who called for help?" one of them asked.

"Yes sir," the groundskeeper called out. "We got us a dead body here."

The younger of the two officers walked up next to us. "You called us to tell us you have a dead body in a cemetery?" His smirk made it obvious he found the situation humorous, too.

"That's enough, Edwards," his partner barked. "This isn't funny."

The four of us gazed down at the dead clown. The older cop cleared his throat, and I wondered if he was reconsidering his statement.

More police and medical personnel began to surround us. Someone put a hand on my shoulder. I turned around to find another police officer staring at me.

"I need you to move back, miss," he said. "Will you come with me?" I followed him to his car. He opened the back door and pointed inside. "Please have a seat. We'll need a statement from you in a little while." He closed the door, and I watched as one of the EMTs from the ambulance knelt next to the grave. His upper body disappeared as he lowered himself into the hole. A few seconds later, he pulled himself back up and shook his head at the law enforcement personnel who stood watching him.

Immediately, they all moved back, and one of the officers began sticking stakes in the ground and running yellow crime scene tape around the grave and the area surrounding it. A couple of men in plain clothes, wearing gloves, rooted around in the dirt. Their efforts suddenly brought home the stark reality of Harold's death. He was a close friend of Adam's, and I'd spent more time around him than most of the other members in the group. A sense of loss washed over me, along with compassion for Harold's family.

I attempted to focus on the police procedures to get my mind off Harold's misfortune. The investigators worked together like a well-oiled machine. This was obviously not their first crime scene. My interest in what they were doing kept me from noticing someone approach the car. I yelped from surprise when I heard a knock on the back window.

I cranked my head around to see Adam staring at me. He came around to the side of the car and opened the door. I jumped out and into his arms.

"Oh, Adam," I said, my voice shaking. "It was awful. Harold lying there, dead. How could this happen?"

"I have no idea," he said. "It. . .it's unbelievable. You said you found him in Bam Bam's grave?"

I pulled back so I could see his face. "Would you please stop calling these men by those ridiculous clown names? I found Harold in Marvin's grave. Calling them Bam Bam and Binky. . .well, it's just not respectful."

Adam frowned. "You don't understand, Hilde. Bam Bam. . . I mean, Marvin, asked for a clown funeral. Calling him by his clown name *is* respectful."

"Well, I don't think Harold asked anyone for a clown funeral—or any other kind of funeral," I snapped as I stepped back. "You know, I've been working hard to get over my fear of clowns. Finding one stone-cold dead isn't helpful." I frowned at him. "That reminds me. Why was he dressed in his costume? The funeral isn't until two."

Adam shrugged. "Maybe he couldn't go home to change before the service. Or maybe he thought he should be in uniform when he delivered Marvin's hat. Your guess is as good as mine."

Before I had a chance to respond, the officer who'd first escorted me to his car strolled up. "Miss," he said, "didn't I ask you to stay in the car?"

If the law enforcement personnel swarming around the gravesite had exhibited any sign of incredulity when they'd first arrived on the scene, it was gone now. The atmosphere was charged with a sense of serious dedication and professionalism. The officer in front of us stared at me without even so much as a hint of humor. He seemed to be about my age and wasn't much bigger than me. It was obvious he didn't suffer fools gladly.

"I'm. . .I'm sorry, Officer," I said, glancing at his badge. "It's Officer Mil–Milk. . .toast?"

His face reddened. "That's Milquest, miss." His eyes moved on to Adam. "And you are?"

"Adam," he said. "Adam Sawyer. I'm a friend of Miss Higgins. And of the dead man."

Officer Milquest's eyebrows shot up. "And which dead man are we talking about? The dead man in the grave now?

Or the dead man who is supposed to be there later today?"

Adam's eyes widened. The officer's no-nonsense attitude was intimidating. "Well, both of them, actually."

The policeman's eyes narrowed. "I understand both men liked to dress up like clowns. Do you participate in this. . . this lifestyle choice?" He spit out the last two words like he'd accidentally bitten into rancid meat and had to get rid of it as quickly as possible.

Adam's face lost most of its color. "L–lifestyle choice?" he sputtered. "For goodness' sakes! We just entertain sick kids, Officer. That's it. It's not like we go around in our costumes all the time. You make us sound. . .well. . ."

"Weird?" Milquest said, only raising one eyebrow this time. "No. Not at all, sir." He pointed to the backseat of the squad car. "If you would both have a seat, please. A detective will be over to take your statements in a few minutes."

I obediently scooted back into the car, yanking on Adam's sleeve to get him to follow me. I had the feeling he wanted to say something else to the policeman—and that no matter what it was, it wasn't going to help anything.

"Adam, just get in the car," I hissed. "Now." Reluctantly, he slid in next to me.

After rolling the windows down a few inches so we wouldn't suffocate, Milquest closed the door and walked away.

Adam shook his head. "I can't believe this. It's a nightmare. Tell me what happened, Hilde."

"I got here a little after nine o'clock," I said. "I almost drove off when I saw Harold's car near the gravesite. I figured he was here to set the hat up. But since he knows my car, I decided I should at least drive over and say hello. When I pulled up behind him, I didn't see anyone, so I got out to look."

"What made you look in the grave?"

I grunted. "It wasn't my original intention. I saw the hat on the headstone, but I couldn't find Harold anywhere. I thought it was odd that the plywood that should have covered the grave was lying against the tree, and the greenery that should have been over it was rumpled up in a heap nearby. It didn't make sense."

Adam sighed. "It's nice to know my girlfriend knows all the ins and outs of funeral procedures."

"You'd be surprised how much rubs off when you have a job like mine."

"And what kind of a job is that?"

A large, basset-faced man in plain clothes bent over outside the car window. Before I could answer, he introduced himself.

"I'm Detective Devereaux. I need to ask you two some questions." He opened the front door of the car and slid into the driver's seat. Then he pulled a notebook and a pen out of his pocket. "Let's take you first, young lady. I understand you found the body?"

"Yes, that's right."

"Your name?"

"Hildegard Bernadette Higgins."

He paused and stared at me for a moment. "Like the saints?"

I nodded. "It's a long story. . . ."

"I'm sure it is," he said, shaking his head. "You mentioned your job had something to do with funerals? Exactly what is it you do?"

"I'm a hairstylist. I work with funeral homes."

He turned around and peered at me through bloodshot eyes. His jowls wiggled when he shook his head. "You're kidding."

"No. I'm serious."

His gaze swung to Adam. "Do you work with dead people, too?"

"No. I'm a stockbroker," Adam said sharply.

I reached over and touched his arm to warn him to watch his attitude.

"Listen, Detective," I said with as much grace as I could, "this is extremely hard on both of us. Especially Adam. He's lost two close friends in the space of four days. I know there are. . .unusual aspects to this situation, but if you could just try to be somewhat sensitive. . ."

Devereaux flushed. "You're right. I apologize. Let's start again, shall we?" He glanced down at his notepad. "Officer Milquest tells me your name is Adam Sawyer, young man? Is that correct?"

Adam nodded.

"And your relationship to the dead man?"

Adam hesitated. "Um. . .well, you see, we're both clowns."

The look on the detective's face made it clear we were in for a very long day.

CHAPTER ⛫ TWO

Adam and I spent at least an hour answering questions at the cemetery. After that, we were driven to the police station to do it all over again. First together and then separately. Finally, a little after one o'clock, Detective Devereaux told me I could leave. The fact that my car was back at the cemetery didn't seem to bother him. I asked about Adam.

"We're not quite finished with Mr. Sawyer," he said gruffly. "Please don't leave the state, Miss Higgins. We may want to talk to you again. But for now, you're free to go."

Although I had no plans to travel, I wondered about his warning. Did they suspect me of something? Was discovering a clown corpse illegal? Not wanting to delay my release, I just smiled and hurried out of the room. Once I reached the hallway, I saw a bench against the wall and sat down. Finding my cell phone in my crowded purse took a couple of minutes. In the meantime, an old grocery list, a key ring with a light I'd gotten at a Gaither Homecoming concert, a small bottle of hand disinfectant, and two pens jumped from my purse and fell out onto the floor in front of me.

Embarrassed, I glanced around, hoping no one had noticed. A quick look at the other people nearby, including a woman in handcuffs and a rough-looking man who was attempting to cheer up his distressed friend by telling him, "It ain't your fault, Dink. The other guy had it comin'," made it clear that they all had their own problems. A skinny girl with a purple streak in her black hair certainly wasn't their top priority.

I picked everything up and jammed it back into my purse, but not before checking out the pens. I have a habit of acquiring pens from other locations. No matter how hard I try to stop it, the problem persists. The first pen was from a local restaurant. No mystery there. I must have picked it up when I signed my debit card receipt. I'd take it back the next time I ate there. The second pen defied explanation. Oliver's Burgers and Bait, Hutchinson, Kansas. Well, at least it was from Kansas—even though I hadn't been to Hutchinson recently. I have pens from almost every state in the union, and I have no earthly idea how some of them found their way into my possession. I figure it's some kind of cosmic joke—God's way of messing with me a little. The only positive result from my humiliating kleptomania came last winter, when a pen I'd accidentally absconded led to the solution of a murder. So it's not all bad.

I sighed and flipped my phone open. Who to call? My mother, a successful neurosurgeon, was probably wrist deep in brains. I decided to try my best friend, Paula. She works as a senior funeral director at Willowbrook, Wichita's nicest funeral home. Even though Mondays were usually busy for her, maybe I could still catch her at lunch. Sometimes she took her break late. I found my directory and located the number for Willowbrook. Then I pushed SEND, and the phone beeped as it dialed the number.

"Willowbrook Funeral Home. This is Paula."

Grateful she'd answered the phone, I explained my problem. Then I explained it again—after she stopped laughing.

"Sorry, Hilde," she sputtered. "There are simply some things you never expect to hear. One is your best friend telling you she's discovered a dead clown in another dead clown's grave. Another one would be that Hilde Higgins has been hauled in to the police station." With that she started to giggle again.

"Excuse me," I interrupted, unable to keep the irritation out of my voice. "I'm happy you're amused, but I'm still stuck down here without a way to get home. Are you coming to get me or not?"

"Wow, I'm sorry, but I don't see how I can leave now. I've got to contact the Martinez family. Sounds like we'll have to reschedule the service. I'm sure the cops won't let us anywhere near the gravesite today. What about your friend Gabe? I doubt he's busy."

She was right about that. Gabriel Bashevis owns a run-down antique store in Eden, Kansas, my hometown. Eden is a few miles outside Wichita—a town so small, only the people who live there know it exists. A couple of farms, a used bookstore, a boardinghouse where I live, and Bashevis Antiques. That's about it.

Gabe had become a good friend last winter after a woman's body had gone missing from a Wichita funeral home. The situation became personal when my integrity and honesty were put into question. Gabe's advice and support endeared him to me. Since his place is right across the street from Mrs. Hudson's, we spend quite a bit of time together. His wisdom has guided me through several situations. He and Adam have also forged quite a bond. Gabe's a recluse, so instead of going out to eat, Adam and I usually end up having dinner at Gabe's house a couple of times a week. The three of us have no trouble talking into the wee hours of the morning.

I wasn't certain Gabe would come get me, but I decided to give it a try. Until a month ago, he didn't even have a phone. My constant pleading finally convinced him to get a cheap cell phone. Unfortunately, as smart as he is, he has a hard time using it. Usually when I call him, his voice mail picks up immediately because he's forgotten to disconnect his last call or charge the phone. Luckily, this time it actually rang and he answered.

"Hello, Hilde. What's up?"

I quickly explained the morning's events and asked if he could possibly come and get me.

"Wh–where did you say you are?"

"The police station downtown."

There was nothing but silence on the line.

"Gabe? Are you there?"

After a few seconds, his subdued voice came through the speaker. "Can you walk down to First Baptist Church? I can pick you up in the parking lot."

Although I wondered what was wrong with the parking lot at the city building, I decided not to question him. I was just thrilled to get a ride. I agreed to meet him at the church.

I put my phone back in my purse, punched the down button on the elevator, and rode to the ground floor with a young man in handcuffs, who was obviously high on something besides life. A grim-faced police officer had a firm grip on his arm. Although this had been an unusually bad day for me, I consoled myself with the knowledge that the man being held prisoner probably had less to look forward to than I did.

I stepped outside to find that although the sky had been clear when I'd entered the building, now it poured down rain. Kansans have a motto: If you don't like the weather, wait a few minutes; it'll change. Wichita was certainly living up to its reputation today.

I zipped up my jacket and considered my options. There were a few buildings between me and my destination. They would afford a little protection from the elements, but they were about a block away, and the parking lot at the church was totally exposed. However, the church shares its lot with the Salvation Army. Surely between the two of them, I'd be allowed to wait inside for Gabe to show up. I mean, Christian charity and all that.

As the downpour grew a little heavier, I wondered if I shouldn't just wait where I was. Surely Gabe would look for me if I wasn't in the parking lot. But I didn't entertain that hope for long. Gabriel Bashevis has his secrets and idiosyncrasies, and he has no intention of explaining them to me now—or ever. For some reason, he didn't want to be seen at the police station. I could stand here and hope he'd change his mind, but I'd be waiting a long, long time.

I'd just decided to make a run for it, get to the church as quickly as I could, and take my chances with the charity thing, when my phone rang. The call was coming from Adam's cell. I stepped back under the protection of the entrance overhang and answered.

"Adam, where are you?"

"I'm upstairs, Hilde. They just released me. Where are you?"

"I'm out front—at the south entrance."

"I'm on my way." He hung up.

Spring in Wichita is still chilly, especially when it rains. I went back inside the building to wait for Adam. My teeth were beginning to chatter. Running through the rain to the parking lot wasn't going to be comfortable. I'd grabbed a light jacket when I'd left the boardinghouse. Obviously, my thicker coat would have been a much better choice.

I walked down the hall until I could see the elevators. After several minutes, Adam still hadn't shown up. I noticed that several times, officers who were escorting prisoners upstairs waved other people away from their elevator. I'm sure it was for their protection, but most of those waiting didn't look very happy about it.

Finally, the doors to one of the elevators opened, and Adam came out. He looked a little disheveled and very upset. I waved at him and he jogged over to me, grabbing me by the arm and pulling me toward the front entrance.

"Hey, wait a minute," I said crossly, pulling my arm away. "I don't like being manhandled."

"I'm sorry, Hilde. I just want out of here."

He hurried toward the doors, pushed them open, and stepped outside. I forgot about being upset and followed him. I'd never seen him this rattled.

"What's wrong with you?" I asked when I finally caught up to him. "I know this has been rough. . . ."

He leaned against the building and ran his hand through his longish dark hair. He stared out at the rain, his blue eyes full of worry. "They think I did it, Hilde."

"Did what?"

His next words made me feel much colder on the inside than I did on the outside.

"They think I killed Harold."

CHAPTER THREE

The ride to Shady Rest Cemetery was markedly quiet. Adam and I were soaked to the skin but thankful the heater in Gabe's old truck warmed us up a little. Crammed three in a seat also helped to keep the cold away. I was in the middle and probably the most comfortable since air blew in through the doors. Gabe kept glancing at us. I tried a couple of times to get Adam to talk about his experience at the police station, but my efforts were to no avail. All he would do is grunt or say, "I don't want to talk about it right now."

I was thinking about grabbing a fistful of his hair and asking him if he'd like to talk about *that*, but we arrived at the cemetery before I could put my plan into action. Gabe's ancient truck rattled through the rows of tombstones like a loose sack of bones. Finally, he stopped next to my car. The crime scene tape was gone, as were all the police officers and investigators. The plywood and the greenery had been put back over the grave, and Marvin's hat had disappeared. Although the area looked relatively normal, extensive tire tracks and small remnants of torn yellow tape remained. It was obvious something had happened here. A quick call to Paula after leaving the station had confirmed that Marvin's funeral was rescheduled for Thursday. I was certain the change had been inconvenient for the family, but allowing a little time to pass after the strange events of today seemed the right thing to do.

I suddenly realized there was something else missing besides the police and the interment that was supposed to be taking place right about now. "Where's your car?" I asked Adam.

"They impounded it."

I felt my mouth drop open. "What? Why?"

"Standard procedure," Gabe said softly. "They'll go over it for evidence. If they don't find any, they'll release it back to him."

Adam had already told me that he was under suspicion, but there was something about his car being taken that made the whole thing seem too real. And ugly.

Adam started to open the door to let me out, but I reached over and grabbed his hand. "Listen, bub," I said as firmly as I could, "you need to talk to us. We know you didn't kill Harold. Unless you open up, we can't possibly help you."

Adam turned toward me. His face was pale and his mouth tight. "Help me? How in the world are you going to help me? The police have evidence that points to me. They think I'm involved."

"They aren't convinced of it, or you'd be in jail," Gabe said, his voice firm but gentle. "They're trying to shake you up, hoping you'll confess. Problem is, it looks like it's working."

I stared at him. "What do you mean it's working? Adam certainly didn't kill Harold."

Gabe blew out a quick breath of air. "I know that, Hilde. But he's acting as guilty as sin. My point is that he needs to quit responding to their tactics."

"And how do I do that?" Adam asked, his voice sharp with indignation. "Laugh and act nonchalant when one of my close friends is murdered and I'm blamed for it? I don't think I can do that."

"Of course he doesn't mean that," I said. "All Gabe is saying is—"

"All Gabe is saying," the elderly man said, interrupting me, "is that you both need to come back to my place." He glanced at his watch. "It's almost two, and neither one of you has had lunch yet. Let's eat and we'll talk this out."

Adam was silent. I reached over and put my hand on his arm. "We're concerned about you, Adam. We're your friends. Lean on us. What if our positions were reversed? Wouldn't you want to help me?"

"Actually, it *was* you, last winter," Gabe said.

"That's right," I said, a little more forcefully. "You stood by me even though I was accused of being a thief—and even worse. You need to trust us now."

Adam's shoulders slumped. "You're right," he said. "I'm sorry, but I've never been hauled into a police station before.

It's hard to know how to act."

Gabe chuckled. "I don't think there's any kind of official etiquette to fall back on. You'll just have to wing it."

"Well, one thing I do know," I said. "We're going to Gabe's to sort this out. I'll make lunch and we'll talk."

"Okay. But I need to go home first to change. These wet clothes don't make me feel any better." He glanced over at Gabe. "Could you give me a ride?"

"I can drive you," I said.

Adam shook his head. "You're making lunch. This will be easier."

"I'd be happy to take you," Gabe said. "You go on, Hilde. We'll meet you back at my place."

I had the uncomfortable feeling that Adam didn't want to go with me because he knew I'd try to get him to talk. Gabe, on the other hand, would be more willing to stay quiet and let Adam stew a bit longer. Men. Closing up emotionally seemed to be a trait they worked hard to perfect.

I pulled Adam's face close to mine and kissed him on the cheek. "I'll have lunch ready about three. How about some of my special sandwiches?"

He smiled for the first time since we'd left the station. "With that great sandwich spread?"

"Yes. I just made some last night."

"And I'll provide some butter cookies and tea," Gabe said.

Adam's eyebrows rose just a smidgen. "Blueberry and

apple tea?"

Gabe cleared his throat. "I'm not sure it would go well with our sandwiches. How about a nice, mild afternoon tea?"

Adam was silent. I pushed slightly against Gabe. He's very fussy about what tea goes with what food, but I cared more about cheering Adam up than I did about inappropriate food and drink combinations. Gabe got my hint.

"We can have the blueberry and apple tea if that's what you want, Adam," he said. I knew him well enough that I could hear the hesitation in his voice. Stepping out of his comfort zone was a big sacrifice for him.

Adam perked up again. "That sounds great. I'm not sure it'll wash away the awfulness of this day, but it will certainly help numb it."

He got out of the car, and I slid out behind him. He gave me a quick hug and then jumped back in. I ran to my car, trying not to get any wetter than I already was. Once inside, I watched Gabe's old truck clatter its way toward the entrance. I followed them, trying to sort out all the feelings brewing inside me. The shock of discovering Harold, being questioned by the police, and Adam being accused of murder had pushed my emotions into overload.

I passed them once we'd both made it to the highway. Gabe would probably scold me for driving too fast. He has two speeds. Slow and slower. I found him to be an enigma. As cautious as an old woman in some areas, he came with a mysterious past that hinted at something much more dangerous. Last year, Mrs. Hudson asked me to give him a packet that had been delivered to her by mistake. Addressed to Gabriel Bastian instead of Bashevis, it came from a hotel in the Ukraine. It was easy for me to pull up a picture of the envelope in my mind since I have what is commonly referred to as a photographic memory. I'd been tempted many times to look up information in the return address on the Internet to see if I could locate the person who'd sent the package. Out of respect for Gabe, I hadn't. Yet.

His reaction when I handed it over to him was frightening, to say the least. I thought he was having a heart attack. Whatever it was that upset him that day could have had serious consequences, since he actually does have a heart condition. Now I make it my business to keep a close eye on him, making sure he doesn't get too upset. Of course, I try to do this without his knowledge. My concern for him would surely be seen as a breach of the privacy he insists upon.

Although his response to receiving the envelope got my attention, I became really suspicious when I accidentally stumbled across its contents. A letter written in French and a picture of Gabe and a woman with the word *MEURTRE* handwritten across it. My only exposure to French was through Monsieur Max, who ran Maximilian's Salon de L'Elegance—Wichita's premier hairdressing salon. I'd worked there until I found my calling—working with customers who couldn't talk back. Max threw French phrases around the same way some people pepper their speech with expletives.

Strange, since he was born and raised in Boise, Idaho. But through my limited experience with Max's French, I knew the word *murder* when I saw it. I think Gabe figured out I'd seen the picture and the letter. I'm not sure how, but he warned me very sternly to drop the issue for good. He also informed me that he had no intention of answering any questions about it. Maybe not, but his admonition couldn't stop me from wondering. Was he a retired secret agent? Or a convicted felon hiding from the law? It was possible I'd never know. A hard fact to accept for someone as nosy as I am.

When I finally arrived in Eden, the rain had let up a little, but the sky was really dark. Off to the west, a large, low cloud, called a "wall cloud," hung ominously over the city of Wichita. Although I'm not an expert on tornadoes, I've watched enough weather forecasts to know that they can build on the back side of formations just like the one I was watching now. If it continued to advance toward our small town, Mrs. Hudson would be ordering everyone down to the basement.

I had a bag of books in the back of my car that my mother wanted me to give to Ida Mae Washington, the elderly woman who runs the Garden of Eden Bookstore. Ida Mae had stacked shelves of used books in her front room, stuck price tags on them, and opened up to the public. Although she doesn't have many customers, she does a steady business with people like me. I love to read, and Ida Mae keeps me stocked with the best in Christian fiction. Mystery and suspense top my list. I spend many evenings cuddled up in my overstuffed chair, my grandmother's quilt to keep me warm, immersed in a novel from Ida Mae's bookstore.

I drove past Mrs. Hudson's and went a block down the street to Ida Mae's. I wanted to get the books to her before the weather got any worse. I pulled into her driveway. A hand-painted sign in the window of Ida Mae's old bungalow read OPEN in shaky, neon pink letters. It was framed between lace curtains and was only a shade or two darker than the house, which needed a new coat of paint. Ida Mae's husband passed away a couple of years ago. I doubted much upkeep had been done since his death. Ida Mae's loneliness after he was gone had spawned the bookstore. And it seemed to help. Her customers are her family now. Gabe visits often, as do Mrs. Hudson and Minnie, another resident of our boardinghouse. Last year, Ida Mae made another friend, Isaiah Sims, an elderly widower who lived at Mrs. Hudson's. Their common love of books had given them lots to talk about. For a while, it seemed as if their friendship might become something even stronger, but unfortunately Isaiah's health deteriorated. His daughter in Illinois moved him into her home. He'd been gone almost a month now. Besides dropping off the books, I wanted to make sure Ida Mae was okay. I knew she missed her friend.

I clicked my electronic keypad twice, unlocking the back door of my black PT Cruiser. My mother gave it to me after she purchased her latest new car. I absolutely love it and am very grateful to finally have a dependable mode of transportation. Before the Cruiser, I was never sure from one day to the next if my old car would start. I'd just lifted the bag from the back when Ida Mae's door swung open.

The wind had strengthened and it whipped my hair into my eyes, so I could barely see the old woman who stood waving from her porch. I leaned into the blast of air and fought my way toward Ida Mae. When I got to the porch, she put her arm around me and guided me through her front door.

"My goodness, it's really blowing up a storm, isn't it?" She pushed the door shut. "Why in the world are you out in this?"

I held out the bag. "My mother asked me to drop these off to you. Another donation from her book club."

"Why, Hilde Higgins. This could have waited. It's not like I have people lined up waiting to buy my books." She chuckled, the soft, brown skin on her face wrinkling with humor. She took the bag from my hands and carried it to a nearby table already overloaded with old volumes. She began removing the contents, oohing and aahing over each one. My mother's club always bought nice hardcover novels, mostly because they knew Ida Mae would get more money for them.

After emptying the bag, she pointed toward a nearby chair. Although her house needed upkeep, her special touches had created a warm, inviting environment. The wooden floors were polished to a high sheen, partially covered with a colorful oval rag rug. Oak shelves full of books had been pushed up against almost every wall. A comfortable-looking couch covered in deep russet velveteen was positioned between two matching chairs and a large coffee table. Ida Mae had created a cozy conversation area where she could sit with visitors and discuss their recent reads, favorite authors, and whatever else seemed important enough to talk about. If it weren't for Ida Mae's desk, positioned in the corner, facing the interior of the room, and the handwritten signs scattered around that exclaimed, EVERYTHING ON THIS SHELF IS $1.00, or MAKE ME AN OFFER!, anyone stepping through the front door would assume this was a rather comfy home—owned by someone with an over-the-edge fascination with reading.

A large calico sheet, used as a curtain, divided the "bookstore" from the adjoining dining room. Except that now there was no dining room. It had been turned into Ida Mae's personal living room. It was her way of keeping her business and private life separate.

"I got several new mysteries in," she declared gleefully, pointing to the shelves labeled MYSTERY. I followed her finger and found some books I hadn't read yet. I carried my selections to her desk.

The old woman ambled over. "How 'bout I fix us both a nice hot cup of cider?" She seated herself in the rickety old chair behind the desk. "We haven't had much time to talk lately."

"I know. I'm sorry," I said with a smile. "I wish I could stay for a while, but I have plans. I'm free tomorrow afternoon though. I could come by around three."

"Oh, that would be lovely." Although Ida Mae was in her eighties, she didn't look it. And when she smiled, she appeared even younger. She'd said more than once, "People get old because they think they're supposed to, Hilde. But when the joy of the Lord is truly your strength, you can be as young as you can stand!"

"Then it's a date."

She laughed softly. "I'm sure it will be the best date I've had in a long, long time." She looked through my stack of books. "That'll be $3.00."

"I still think you should charge more," I said while I dug around in my purse. "I'd be paying ten times that at one of the retail stores."

She shook her head. "I need the money—don't get me wrong. But the main reason I do this is so I can pass good books along. Doesn't do anyone any good when great stories sit on bookstore shelves not being read."

We'd had this conversation more than once. And every time she said the same thing. I might as well learn to save my breath; she wasn't going to change. Her happiness meant more to me than anything else, and although she wasn't wealthy, she was perfectly happy. She'd endured the death of a spouse and spent more time alone than she wanted to, but she was still content. I thought about Paul's declaration in Philippians—that he'd learned to be content and rejoice whatever his condition. I was convinced that because Ida Mae didn't rely on circumstances to give her joy, she was able to walk in God's peace. It emanated from her. I could even feel it inside her home. If one could gather every book in the world, sell them for their full retail price, and pocket the money, they still wouldn't have anything as precious as what Ida Mae had found. True contentment.

She placed my books in the bag I'd brought with me, gave me a hug, and sent me on my way with a warning to keep an eye on the weather. When I stepped outside, I could see that her words were not to be taken lightly. The wall cloud had darkened and was moving over Wichita. Lightning streaked from it like electric tentacles. Although the rain in Eden was nothing more than a drizzle now, it was obvious that the approaching storm held copious amounts of moisture.

I jumped in my car and drove down the street to the board-inghouse, parking under the small covered space on the west side of the large Victorian structure. I looked across the street and saw Gabe's truck already parked in the driveway. He must have cranked it up a bit, probably so he could beat the storm. I was certain Adam had brought Watson, our dog, along with him. I call him ours even though he lives with Adam. Dogs aren't allowed at Mrs. Hudson's, although she doesn't mind when Watson comes to visit. In fact, she's rather partial to him. Most people are. Watson is a friendly little pug who loves everyone he meets. He used to belong to a woman named Mabel Winnemaker. After Mabel died, Watson ended up at the pound. Adam rescued him, and he's been ours ever since. Once bothered by asthma, Watson now takes medication that helps to control it. He's about the happiest dog I've ever known. Probably because he's spoiled rotten. Adam and I are bad enough, but Gabe treats him like a visiting dignitary, feeding him food I might consider even too good for me. Watson goes everywhere, even to work with Adam. The partners in his office built a small fenced area with a doghouse behind their building where he spends his weekdays—unless he's running around inside, visiting the staff and getting stuffed with doggy treats. He's become the office mascot. I've never heard of a brokerage house with a mascot, but then again, most dogs aren't Watson.

And Adam's clown friends have been training the funny little dog to be part of their act. He looks so comical with his silly hat and ruffled collar, trying to learn the different commands they give him, so he can entertain sick children right along with his human companions. All in all, Watson's life is better than most humans'. Even though he lost his best friend last winter, he's made a whole bunch of new ones. He's especially bonded with Adam. I don't know if he thinks Adam is his dad—but he's certainly treated like a most beloved child.

I ran upstairs to my room, made sandwiches, sliced some apples, and packed everything into my picnic basket. I hurried as fast as I could so I wouldn't get caught in the basement with Mrs. Hudson and her nephew, Derek. He was arrested for drug possession last year, no small thanks to me, and spent some time in jail. Although he seems to have turned a corner, I've caught him looking at me strangely more than once. I'm not sure what his odd glances mean, and I'm not really interested in finding out.

Before I left to go to Gabe's, I fed the only pet I'm allowed to have at Mrs. Hudson's. Sherlock, my goldfish, had been my personal confidant for quite some time—until Adam and Gabe came along. Adam's encouragement to get a larger home for Sherlock had moved him from his big, round bowl to a small aquarium with an air pump and a little castle he likes to swim through. He certainly seems happier in his new surroundings. In fact, when Adam and I first transferred him, he seemed absolutely giddy. Or as giddy as a goldfish gets. I felt a little guilty about not giving him more spacious living quarters before, but I had it in my mind that aquariums were for tropical fish—not plain old goldfish. Although actually, nothing about Sherlock is plain. He's big and beautiful—and he listens to me when I talk. At first Adam didn't believe me when I told him about my goldfish's listening skills. But he's seen Sherlock swim up to the side of his tank and stare at me when I speak to him. Now he's a reluctant believer. And Adam has also seen Sherlock wave his fin at me. In fact, he's waved at Adam a few times, causing my down-to-earth boyfriend a little consternation. "If this fish belonged to anyone else," he said to me, "I'd think it was my imagination. But if there is anyone on earth who could train a goldfish to wave, it would be you, Hilde Higgins."

I said good-bye to Sherlock and glanced once around my room before leaving. I love my apartment. I live on the top floor in a space that was actually part of the attic until it was converted into an apartment. I have an old iron bed that creaks reassuringly when I roll over in the night. There are four large windows in the front of the room. I love to sit on my window seat and gaze at the stars. It's amazing how many can be seen when you're away from the lights of the city. The sky looks like it's been scattered with thousands of sparkling diamonds. Other times, I sit and watch the spring rains wash everything clean. Or in winter, big, fluffy flakes of snow drift past my windows and cover my world with a blanket of white while I sip hot tea. Even Gabe's old house looks good wrapped in snow. I eat my meals at a built-in booth tucked into a nook in my small but cozy kitchen. There's a big walk-in closet with a lace curtain instead of a door and a comfortable overstuffed chair made of gold and purple paisley fabric with a matching ottoman.

I read the books I pick up from Ida Mae in my chair, while an antique brass lamp illuminates the pages. Since it is the only real light in the room besides the windows and a low-wattage bulb in the ceiling, every evening my room has a special ambience that I adore. My mother calls it depressing and spooky. I call it perfect.

I glanced out the windows once more before closing the door and heading down the stairs. The sky had a strange, greenish glow. This phenomenon is something odd that happens in the spring in Kansas. It seems to occur before or after hail. I decided to leave my PT under the covered parking area Mrs. Hudson has set up for her tenants. It's really nothing more than a tin roof on metal poles, but it has saved my car from dings and dents more than once. I walked to Gabe's since it's right across the street, but unfortunately, the dirt road had turned to mud from all the rain. By the time I stepped up onto his porch, my old leather boots were caked with sludge. I pushed the door open, set my basket down, and slid my boots off onto the mat Gabe keeps there. My old boots have been through a lot, and they were starting to look like it.

Gabe was nowhere in sight. However, I was certain he knew I was there. He has a camera set up on his front porch. A little alarm rings in his apartment when someone approaches his door. He says it's so he won't have to sit downstairs all day, but since he never has any customers anyway, his explanation doesn't make much sense. It simply adds to the enigma that is Gabe Bashevis.

I picked up my basket and made my way through the old antiques store. Neglected pieces of pottery and glass gathered dust on mismatched shelves lined up around the room. A life-size stuffed bear stood in one corner, his paws extended. On one leg were several women's purses—probably from the forties and fifties. On the other leg, an array of printed scarves were draped near his paw, making him look like a desperate salesman trying to rid himself of his wares. I waved at him. I'd grown rather fond of the poor old thing.

I trudged slowly up the stairs, leaving a world of darkness and shadows for the bright and beautifully furnished apartment where Gabe actually lives. How he pays for all his lovely furniture and state-of-the-art appliances is anyone's guess. Except for mine. Guessing out loud about Gabe is forbidden, so I keep my opinions and questions to myself.

"Anyone here?" I said loudly as I stepped into the living room. Gabe's upstairs is nothing like his downstairs. Beautiful wooden floors, large Oriental rugs, and soft leather furniture display his style and exceptional taste. Over a large stone fireplace hangs a painting of a beautiful landscape with rolling hills and massive oak trees that line a sparkling blue river. And in his dining room, there's a carved mahogany table and chairs with a matching buffet. On the wall is a portrait of a woman with sad eyes. The painting is hauntingly beautiful and somewhat disturbing. Every time I look at it, I feel as if I want to find a way to bring a smile to the woman's face.

Before Adam called out, "In the kitchen!" the sound of doggy nails tapping across the floor announced that Watson was on his way to greet me. He ran from the kitchen as fast as his short little legs could carry him. Watson is almost all blond except for black trimming on his ears and muzzle.

And his eyes look as if someone outlined them with mascara. When he's happy, he wags his tail so hard his whole rear end wiggles. It's amazing that he stays on his feet. As he ran toward me, his mouth was open in a wide grin and his tongue hung out one side, making him look somewhat deranged. This was par for the course. I put my basket down and dropped to my knees, holding my hands out. He jumped up into my arms, covering my face with doggy kisses. Whenever Gabe witnesses this behavior, he always shakes his head and mentions other places dogs like to lick. Then he hands me a washcloth. But today he stayed in the kitchen, so the only telltale sign that I'd been kissed would come from any remaining saliva on my face. I hugged the affectionate dog once more and then picked up my basket and headed for the kitchen, Watson following closely behind.

I found Adam and Gabe deep in conversation, their voices low and serious. Gabe looked at me, sighed, got up, and handed me a paper towel that he moistened under the faucet for a moment. I obediently cleaned off my face while he put my basket on the counter and opened it.

"Looks great, Hilde," he said.

"I haven't been the least bit hungry," Adam interjected, "but the idea of one of your SPAM salad sandwiches makes my stomach gurgle."

As if acknowledging his words, a strange rumbling sound emitted from his middle region, causing Gabe and me to laugh.

I sat down in a chair across from Adam while Gabe put

our food on the table. Then he sat down, poured us each a cup of hot tea, and said a blessing over our meal.

"So bring me up to speed. Why do the police think you killed Harold?" I took a big bite of my sandwich and waited for his answer.

Adam stared straight at me and said, "Well, the main reason they suspect me seems to be because the groundskeeper saw me do it."

CHAPTER FOUR

There are very few things in life that could cause me to spit out a bite of a SPAM salad sandwich. The crunchy sweet pickles combined with mayonnaise, hard-boiled eggs, celery, onions, and garlic powder give the yummy meat just the right flavor. As good as it is, however, it doesn't look as appetizing when you spew it out on the table.

"For crying out loud, Hilde," Gabe huffed. He's very particular about his home. For an old man, he sure can move fast. He was on his feet and cleaning up my mess within seconds. Wiping up chunks of SPAM salad with one hand and pounding me on the back to save me from choking showed impressive dexterity. I wanted to thank him, but I was too busy coughing up the rest of my big bite. My mother's admonition about "eating in a more ladylike manner" rang in my ears. Thankfully, she wasn't here to watch me reap the results of ignoring her advice.

Finally, the coughing subsided and Gabe ceased his domestic attention to my embarrassing reaction. I turned my attention back to my startled and probably somewhat grossed-out boyfriend.

"What do you mean, the groundskeeper saw you do it?" I rasped.

Adam raised one eyebrow and stared at me with consternation. "What I mean is that he told the police he saw my car at the cemetery right around the time Harold was killed."

Adam had recently traded in his black Lexus for a bright red Saturn. His job as a stockbroker had made him a little unsure of future economic trends, and getting a car with lower payments seemed the right thing to do. To me, he hadn't lost anything. His new car was sporty and attractive. And its bright color seemed more consistent with his personality. I mean, how many clowns would be caught dead in a black Lexus?

"But you weren't there, were you?"

Now Adam raised the other eyebrow. "Yes, I was there, Hilde. I actually murdered Harold. You caught me. And here I thought I'd gotten away with it. I guess it was your top-notch detective skills that caused my downfall." He shook his head and chomped down on his sandwich.

I sighed. "You don't have to get snotty. I know you didn't kill Harold. I'm just asking if you went by to check out the gravesite. Maybe to make sure the hat was where it was supposed to be."

He put his sandwich down. "No, of course not. You said you would follow up, and I trust you. The groundskeeper. . . I believe they said his name is Clarence Diggs—"

I held up my hand. "Wait a minute. You are *not* telling

me that the guy who works at the cemetery is named Mr. Diggs. You can't mean it."

Adam frowned at me. "Why wouldn't his name be. . ." The light obviously went on somewhere in his head. "Oh, I get it. Mr. Diggs. Funny." But he didn't laugh—or look amused. However, I heard Gabe snort. He got a kick out of it even if Adam wasn't in the mood to see the humor.

"As I was saying," Adam said a little forcefully, "Mr. Diggs said he saw my car parked near Marvin's grave a little before eight o'clock. His shift starts at eight."

"You're driving that new red car, right?" Gabe said.

"Yes. But I was home at eight, and so was my car."

"Can anyone verify that?" Gabe asked.

Adam pointed at Watson, who was lying in the corner snoring so loud we had to raise our voices a tad. I envied him. There were no problems in his world. "I was with Watson until Hilde called me. He's the only one who can vouch for me."

Gabe stared intently at him. "What about the neighbors? Would any of them have noticed you? Or seen your car?"

Adam shook his head slowly. "No, I don't think so. The car was in the garage, and I didn't see anyone when I left."

A thought struck me. "Wait a minute. You asked me to check out Marvin's gravesite because you had a meeting this morning and couldn't do it. Why were you home?"

He shrugged. "The appointment was canceled. You'd already left, so I decided to go into the office late. I spent several hours last night going over a client's portfolio, and I was tired."

It made sense, so why did a little wiggle of doubt try to push its way into my brain? "So the caretaker. . .Mr. Diggs, saw a red car at the gravesite around eight o'clock? That's it? There are thousands of red cars in Wichita. How in heaven's name can they even begin to suspect you?"

"When I got to the cemetery, after you called me, Mr. Diggs told the police that my car looked a lot like the car he saw this morning." Adam sighed. "Unfortunately, that's not all of it. Harold's appointment book was lying on the seat of his vehicle. Supposedly, he'd written 'Adam, 7 a.m.' on today's page."

"'Adam, 7 a.m.'? That could mean anything. Maybe he was trying to remind himself that you wanted him to take the hat to the cemetery this morning, and he was going to do it at seven. How can they use that to tie you to his murder?"

"Because, Hilde," Gabe interjected, the humor gone from his face, "someone said they saw Adam's car there around the time Harold was murdered. And it looked like they had an appointment." He picked up the teapot sitting on the table and refilled his cup. Then he put it back down slowly. "I hate to say it, but it doesn't look good. Right now, you must be their primary suspect."

Adam's mouth dropped open. I was thankful he'd swallowed his last piece of sandwich. "But I didn't do it!"

Gabe smiled at him. "I know that, but it's important

that you understand how the police see this. All the circumstantial clues so far direct them toward one person. You. We hope they'll look at other suspects. Or they might try to find additional evidence that ties you to the murder. Their main focus will be to search for forensic proof that points specifically to you. I believe they told you there was a shovel lying on top of Harold?"

Adam nodded. "At one point, one of the detectives wanted to get me to confess, I guess. He told me that he knew I'd hit poor Harold with a shovel and then threw it in the grave after I dumped his body into it."

"Then they'll be going over that shovel with a fine-tooth comb, looking for fingerprints, DNA, anything that could tie you to the crime."

"Well, they won't find anything," Adam huffed.

"Where did the shovel come from?" Gabe asked me. "I thought they use a backhoe now to dig graves."

"Either that or an excavator," I said. "But good old shovels are still used around cemeteries. The groundskeeper takes care of the grass, trees, and plants just like you would—if you actually ever did that sort of thing." Since Gabe rarely poked his head outside, tending his yard was out of the question. His house was surrounded by dirt and weeds.

He ignored my obvious dig. "They'll also be looking for motive. Did you have any reason to want Harold dead?"

Adam turned ashen. "Of course not. He was my friend. That's ridiculous."

The look on his face started warning bells ringing wildly in my mind. I looked at Gabe. His expression told me that he'd noticed something amiss in Adam's reaction, too.

"Adam," Gabe said slowly, "if there was something wrong between you and Harold, you need to tell us now. We can't help you if you're not honest with us."

Adam picked up his cup and took a big gulp. We almost had another dining disaster. The tea was incredibly hot, and his previously pasty white complexion gave way to something akin to an overly ripe tomato. But to his credit, he swallowed the searing liquid.

It took a bit for him to catch his breath and get down the cup of cold water Gabe quickly poured for him. After finishing off the water, he put the cup down and stared at us for several seconds before speaking. "Look," he said carefully, "this is between us. It can't go any further than this room."

"If this is that 'client privilege' excuse, it won't work this time, Adam," Gabe said with a frown. "Your client is dead and you're involved in a murder. Trust me, the police won't accept it. If there is any kind of motive for killing Harold, the police will find it."

Adam dropped his head into his hands for a few seconds. I could almost hear the gears turning in his brain. Finally, he looked up and offered us a rather sick-looking smile. "You know, this is silly. In all the years I've known Harold, we've always been good friends. The one time in our lives we have a problem, he winds up dead. It's the most ridiculous timing."

Gabe snorted. "Murder is never convenient. Generally, people don't plan for it. That's why alibis are almost always hard to find, and clues can easily point in the wrong direction. Murder is sloppy. Sometimes solving it is nothing more than clearing away the things that don't make sense."

"When you have eliminated the impossible, whatever remains, however improbable, must be the truth," I muttered.

"You obviously know your Sherlock Holmes," Gabe said.

I nodded. "Hopefully, Sherlock's wisdom will help us prove Adam had nothing to do with Harold's death."

He sighed. "Well, I think we'd better keep Sherlock in the background for now." He turned to Adam. "Back to the reason you had to kill Harold."

Adam hesitated. "Let me make this as clear as I can. I had no reason whatsoever to kill Harold." At Gabe's threatening look, he continued. "Okay, okay. If someone wanted to find a motive, it would probably have something to do with Harold's accusation that I was stealing money from his account. He approached me last week and asked about his portfolio. The volatility in the stock market had affected his account negatively. He was down several thousand dollars. I tried to explain that it would improve, but he didn't want to listen to me. He started accusing me of taking his money." Adam shook his head. "I couldn't believe it. To be honest, I didn't even know what to say. He stormed out of my office, threatening to go to my boss and demand an investigation. That's the reason I asked you to check about Marvin's hat, Hilde. I'd left a message with Harold's son, Donnie, asking him to make certain the hat was there before the service. Harold never called me back, and I was too uncomfortable to talk to him directly."

"Wow," I said. "You and Harold were so close. I can't believe he'd suspect you of taking his money. That doesn't sound like him."

Adam shrugged. "That's exactly what I'm saying. He was already upset when he came into my office that day. Something else was bothering him, but I have no idea what it was."

"It's important we find that out," Gabe said. "It might be the real motive." He frowned at me. "When we clear away the impossible—that Adam killed Harold—whatever we're left with will be the truth. Your Sherlock quote applies here, but our problem is that the police don't know Adam. They can't dismiss him as a suspect. Right now they have circumstantial evidence, and if they find out about Harold's suspicions, they'll be able to add motive to it. And without an alibi. . ."

Before Gabe could finish his sentence, a rather loud alarm sounded. I jumped and almost spilled my tea. Adam looked around like he was expecting a SWAT team to pour into the room, guns blazing.

"Relax," Gabe said, rising from his chair. "It's my weather radio. You two stay here while I check to see what's going on."

I tried moving my feet a little since one of them was going numb, but Watson was busy using it for a pillow and didn't seem willing to give it up. After a little gentle prodding, he finally wiggled over to the other foot. When I looked up, I found Adam staring at me.

"You do believe that I had nothing to do with killing Harold, don't you?" he said.

"Of course I do!" I exclaimed. "How could you even ask me that?"

"I. . .I don't know. Just a feeling." His sapphire-colored eyes searched mine. "It's like you're seeing me differently, Hilde. You're looking past me. Not at me."

I got up from my chair, displacing my sleepy dog, circled the table, and wrapped my arms around him. "You're imagining things. Don't get paranoid. I've known you since we were kids. You couldn't hurt a fly." I kissed the top of his head. "We can't let this situation drive a wedge between us. Gabe and I intend to do everything we can to help you. You've got to trust us, though."

He grabbed my hand. "You two aren't actually detectives, you know," he said, his tone a little lighter. "I'm not sure you can uncover the truth any better than the police. I know you helped solve Mabel's murder, but you were personally involved in that situation."

"And I'm personally involved in this one," I said softly. "Whatever affects you affects me."

He was silent for several seconds. "I love you, Hildegard Higgins. Do you know that?"

I felt my heart flutter. We'd never said those three little

words to each other, even though we'd hinted around at them. Before I had a chance to respond, Gabe came back into the room. His usual relaxed smile was gone, replaced by a tight frown and narrowed eyes.

"There's a tornado warning for portions of Butler County. It looks like it's headed our way. We need to get down to the basement. Now."

Going to the basement during a tornado warning isn't unusual in Kansas. I'd spent many hours in various basements listening to the radio and waiting for the inevitable all clear. Although I'd seen firsthand the terrible destruction caused by tornadoes, I'd never actually been caught in one. After a while, so many false alarms tend to make you somewhat lackadaisical toward them. But something in Gabe's face made me jump to my feet and grab Watson without asking questions.

"I didn't know you had a basement," Adam said as we followed Gabe down the stairs.

"Don't use it except for laundry and storage," he replied in quick, clipped tones. "Mostly for storage."

When we reached the ground floor, Gabe took a quick left turn and circled around and behind the stairs. There, in the wall, was a door that was so well concealed, at first glance you wouldn't have thought it was anything more than part of the permanent structure. Gabe pulled on a small knob and swung the door open. He stepped inside the opening and yanked on a string hanging from a lightbulb. A stairway appeared out of the darkness.

"Come on," he said to Adam and me. "Get down there. I'll wait here and close the door behind us."

The steps looked pretty rickety. Adam reached over and took Watson from my arms so I could hold on to a rather decrepit wooden railing attached to the wall. Watson grunted as he settled into Adam's grasp. The look of confusion on his face almost made me want to giggle. He was probably wondering just what kind of strange game this was. I'm certain he would rather have been playing with his ball or one of his squeaky toys.

I trailed slowly behind Adam, gingerly putting one stockinged foot in front of the other. Although the bulb at the top of the stairs made it possible to see the steps in front of us, the room below was as black as night.

"Adam, the light switch is directly to your right," Gabe called out while closing the door.

Adam fumbled around until I heard a click—then light blazed forth, flooding the basement. I stepped forward, quickly followed by Gabe. The space was pretty typical— cement walls, lots of stuff in boxes, ancient furniture and tools stacked up against the walls, and that musty smell every old, unfinished basement seems to have. The gardening implements looked like they'd been there quite a while. That certainly explained the unkempt grounds around the old building. However, this didn't seem like the time to chide Gabe for his lack of landscaping skills. Against one wall sat

Gabe's washer and dryer. Sleek and modern, just like the rest of his appliances. Next to them were shelves that held the necessary soap and supplies any laundry space should have.

The only things that looked oddly out of place were five large metal cabinets about six feet high and four feet across. Each one was secured with a huge padlock. What in the world could one old man have that needed that much security?

I turned around to find Gabe staring at me. He didn't say a word, but the slight shake of his head told me I had no choice but to add this anomaly to my growing list of subjects we couldn't talk about. However, the sudden gust of wind that roared over us, shaking the house, drove the questions from my mind.

Gabe pulled three old wooden chairs out of a stack in the corner and pushed them toward us. "Better sit down. We might be here awhile." He turned up the radio he'd brought down with him, and we listened to the forecaster tell us a tornado had been spotted on the ground and was headed our way. Adam put Watson on the floor, but he ignored all the interesting new smells around him, forgoing his usual interest in sniffing everything in sight. He wasn't fond of thunder, and the wind was obviously distressing him, too. He wiggled his way under Adam's chair, his ears down and his tail tucked between his legs.

Adam reached over and took my hand. For some reason I had an urge to pull it away. The awkwardness in the kitchen came back to me. I'd wanted to tell Adam I loved him, too, but the words had stuck in my throat, almost as if they didn't want to come out. I couldn't shake an uneasy feeling. My nose for mystery told me something was wrong. All the clues from Harold's murder pointed toward Adam. I had to ask myself if I really knew this man well enough to believe in his innocence on pure faith alone. We'd been friends as children, but a lot of years had passed. People change. As much as I hated to admit it to myself, I wasn't sure about him. I detested the thoughts that bombarded my mind, but I couldn't force them out. Somewhere inside me was a lingering seed of doubt.

"Citizens in the outlying areas of southeast Wichita are advised to take shelter immediately." The forecaster's voice had taken on an even more ominous tone. "A tornado has been spotted near Prairie Creek Road and Southwest 150th. Residents in this area should take cover immediately."

I reached down and pulled Watson out of his hiding place, holding him tightly against my chest. "That's us," I said, trying to keep the panic out of my voice.

As if confirming my statement, a loud sound that reminded me of an approaching train filled the air around us. The house shook, and for an odd moment, it felt like the building itself inhaled deeply and held its breath. I'd never experienced anything like it before. Adam squeezed my hand and started to pray. Getting my focus off the storm and remembering that God is my true shelter helped to drive away the fear that tried to grip me. God had always protected me against the storms of life. He would protect me against this one, too.

Almost as quickly as it had come, the wind dissipated, and we were surrounded by silence. I started to get up, but Gabe grabbed my arm.

"Sit down." He barked the words out, almost as an order.

Feeling rather chastised, I plopped back down in my chair. Watson began wriggling around, trying to break free of my grip. "Shhhh," I whispered into his ear. "It's okay. Everything's going to be okay."

"I'm sorry, Hilde," Gabe said, patting my shoulder. "The quiet means we're in the eye. The other side of the storm hasn't hit yet."

On cue, that strange train sound began again. As before, the building began to quiver. But this time, I wasn't as frightened. God's promises of peace in the midst of turmoil surrounded me with a palpable sense of safety. Within a couple of minutes, things became quiet again.

"Is that it?" I asked.

Gabe chuckled. "Unless there's another one following behind it, we're in the clear."

"Does that happen very often?" Adam's voice was steady, but his eyes were wide with alarm.

Gabe flashed him a reassuring smile. "I'm not a tornado expert, but I don't think so. I've never seen it."

Within a few minutes, the voice of the weather announcer confirmed that the tornado had moved away from Eden and was going back up into the clouds. He also announced that he was getting reports of damage. I was grateful we were okay, but what about our neighbors?

"We've got to see if everyone's all right," I said.

Gabe stood up and headed for the stairs. "Stay behind me. And don't put Watson down. I don't want him to step on broken glass or anything that might hurt him."

Adam reached his arms out for the trembling dog, and I handed him over. He may not be big, but he can certainly get heavy after a while. Adam and I followed Gabe up the stairs, not certain what awaited us on the other side of the door.

Gabe pushed it open slowly then stepped out. "Everything looks fine," he said, relief in his voice.

Sure enough, the shop was just as dusty and forlorn as usual. The first thing I looked for was my old friend. Mr. Bear stood in his usual place, his arms still offering his outdated goods.

Gabe hurried away to check out his apartment. Adam and I waited at the bottom of the stairs. After a few moments, he reappeared and started down toward us.

"Everything's okay," he said, relief on his face. "I've got a busted window, but that's it. I'll put something across it later. We need to get outside. It looks like some of our neighbors didn't fare as well."

My thoughts went to Sherlock. If anything had happened to him. . .

"The boardinghouse looks fine, Hilde," Gabe said as if

reading my thoughts. "Some of the yard decorations have been tossed about a bit. Looks like part of the fence is gone and quite a few shingles are off the roof." He shook his head. "The worst of it seems to be at Ida Mae's place. I'm afraid she's lost more than just some shingles."

I put Watson down and told him to stay. With all the debris scattered around, it wasn't safe for him outside. He tried to rush the door, but I gently pushed him back. "You stay here, young man," I said sternly. "We'll be back in a bit."

He sat down and gave me his "I'm being abused" look. I knew it was designed to make me feel bad. Usually, it just made me laugh. But concern for Ida Mae drove away any feelings of humor.

The three of us stepped outside to find a huge mess. Although Gabe was right about there not being any serious damage at Mrs. Hudson's, everything that wasn't tied down had been flung around like dead leaves in the wind. The roof had been blown off the carport, but thankfully, the cars seemed fine. All in all, Eden had come through the storm in pretty good shape.

Then I turned toward Ida Mae's bookstore. The roof of the old woman's house was completely gone.

CHAPTER FIVE

The three of us tramped through the mud toward Ida Mae's, threading our way through the debris that covered almost every square foot. But even before we reached her house, the old woman stepped out her front door. As we approached her porch, I could see the confused look on her face.

"Ida Mae, are you okay?"

She reached a trembling hand out toward me. "Yes, honey," she said. "But, oh my, the wind was so loud. I just prayed for God's protection. He took good care of me."

I grabbed her hand and wrapped my arm around her shoulders. Her thin body shook. I looked at Adam. "Get that chair, please. She needs to sit down."

Adam picked up a chair lying in the front yard that had been blown off Ida Mae's porch. He looked for a place that was fairly free of clutter, and I guided Ida Mae to a spot several yards away from her house. It didn't look very stable. I wanted her to stay back in case the walls collapsed.

"Why don't you rest for a little while?" I said. "You've

been through a lot."

By this time, Mrs. Hudson and Minnie had come out the boardinghouse. I didn't see Derek at first, but he must have exited shortly after them. The three of them surveyed the damage while I helped Ida Mae into her chair.

"Oh my," she said, after she had the chance to look around. "That storm really raised a ruckus. Is everyone all right?"

"We're all fine," Gabe said. "But I'm afraid your roof is gone."

Ida Mae's smile crinkled her face. "I kind of figured that out when I looked up at the ceiling in my living room and saw the sky."

I was relieved to hear a little more strength in her voice. Her usual jovial mood had made a comeback, too.

We were all silent as she surveyed the damage. The air around us was incredibly still, and the sky to the east was so dark it was almost black. Yet behind us, the sun peeked out from behind gray clouds. It seemed almost impossible that a violent storm had passed through here only a short time ago. If it hadn't been for the destruction that surrounded us, I'd have had a hard time believing it.

Mrs. Hudson sidled up next to me. "Oh Hilde, I was so worried about you. At first I wasn't sure where you were, but then Derek told me he'd seen you go across the street to Mr. Bashevis's before the storm hit. I knew he would keep you safe." She batted her eyelashes several times at Gabe.

Recently, Mrs. Hudson had decided that Gabe Bashevis was "a catch." I wasn't sure why. As far as she knew, he ran a very unsuccessful antiques store—and that was it. Of course, Gabe happened to be very handsome. Availability and good looks seemed to breed attraction. Unfortunately for her, Gabe wasn't having any of it.

He cleared his throat. "Yes, well, as you can see, we're all fine."

A large red truck came driving slowly up the road. It got as close as it could without running over the scattered wreckage. Butch Appleby, a farmer who lived a little way up the main road, got out and began weaving his way through the remnants of Ida Mae's roof.

"Just wanted to check on you all," he said as he approached us. "Had some damage at the farm, but it ain't too bad. Looks like you folks took the brunt of it."

"I guess it could have been worse," Gabe said. "Ida Mae's place is going to take some work, though." He smiled kindly at her. "You need to get in touch with your insurance agent right away. The inside of your house is exposed. It needs to be covered up until a new roof can be put on."

Ida Mae's thin hand fluttered to her mouth. "Insurance? William took care of all that. I—I don't remember paying for any insurance."

My heart sank as I surveyed the damage to the little house—and to her bookstore.

"We have to find out about that insurance, Ida Mae,"

Gabe said, patting her on the shoulder. "Do you have a place where you keep your papers?"

"Everything's in my desk drawer," she said with a small smile. "I'm afraid my filing system isn't very complicated. There are two shoe boxes—one for my bills and one for important papers." She started to pull herself up. "I'll see if I can find—"

Gabe pushed her down gently. "Why don't you let me get them? I won't look inside the boxes. I'll just bring them to you."

She settled back down in the old wooden chair. "That would be lovely. Thank you. I still feel a little shaky." She shook her head. "Shame on me for allowing fear to come on me like this." She looked up at me. "My mind and heart are calm and fixed on Him, but my body seems to have a will of its own. It's the strangest thing. . . ."

"And perfectly normal," I said. "It's not every day we experience a tornado firsthand. My chest was pounding pretty hard for a while, but I'm better now."

For the first time, I remembered Gabe's heart. I studied him closely, but he appeared to be perfectly fine, steady as a rock. Strange. A tornado didn't bother him, but a package from another country caused a reaction I didn't ever want to see again. I might work with dead people, but watching someone die isn't something I ever want to do. Especially someone I care about.

Gabe started toward the house, but Adam stopped him.

"We're not sure how sound the house is structurally. If you're going in, I'm going with you."

"I'm headed back to the farm to get PeeWee," Butch said. "We need to start clearing out some of this stuff so you folks can walk around a little safer."

PeeWee, Butch's son, certainly didn't fit his nickname. He was over six feet tall and had to be somewhere around three hundred and fifty pounds. He was a kind young man who loved his father and mother and worked hard on their farm. I didn't know the Applebys well, but in a town as small as Eden, it's impossible not to be acquainted with your neighbors. Butch and PeeWee were always good to share some of their corn crop with all of us each year. They'd spoiled me for corn on the cob from any other source. Their corn was so sweet and juicy it was good enough for a main course. It had been front and center more than once in my summer meal planning.

"I'll help, too."

Derek had come up silently behind us. I jumped involuntarily when he spoke. When I turned around, I found him staring at me, his sky blue eyes boring into mine. He pushed a strand of sandy blond hair out of his eyes and offered a tentative smile. Why did I always feel there was something hiding behind his interest in me? And he was interested. Watching me had become one of his hobbies, and frankly, it was getting on my nerves.

Butch slapped him on the back, causing him to almost fall

into me. He reached out and grabbed me, trying to steady himself.

I pushed him back and stepped away. "Get your hands off me, Derek," slipped out of my mouth before I could stop it.

He colored with embarrassment. Then he turned his back on me completely and told Butch he'd wait for him on the front porch. Without saying another word, he walked away from us. I could tell by the way his shoulders slumped that I'd offended him. I wasn't sure how to feel. I hadn't meant to hurt his feelings, but the harm his past antics had caused his aunt and the other residents in the boardinghouse were hard to forget. Mrs. Hudson started to follow him but stopped near a pile of rubble and began to pick through it. I watched her pull up something that looked like the leg of the ceramic deer that had been in her front yard. She shook her head and started sifting through the rest.

"You know, honey," Ida Mae said softly, after Butch walked away, "sometimes people just need us to see them the way God does. He doesn't hold our past mistakes against us."

"I know that, Ida Mae," I said, frowning at her. "But I'm not interested in Derek. I'm dating Adam. Encouraging him to think there could be something between us would be wrong."

Her mouth twitched with humor. "So you think he's got the hots for you, huh?"

Her comment caught me off guard and I laughed. "Why,

Ida Mae Washington, where did you pick up that expression?"

"Pshaw," she said, grinning, "you young people think us old people don't know anything. One of these days, when you get a little older, you just might figure out how smart we really are."

I could have told her that saying "pshaw" kind of ruined her new cool image, but I didn't have the heart. "I get the feeling there's something you think I should know. Just what is it?"

She rubbed her hands together and stared off into the distance for a moment. "I usually never tell anyone what my customers buy, but I'm going to make an exception in this case, honey. You must keep this to yourself, though."

I wasn't sure selling books was akin to the expectation patients have toward privacy between themselves and their doctors. In fact, I could remember a time when she'd divulged to me the kind of books Gabe liked to read, but this situation seemed to be different. My curiosity was certainly aroused.

"I won't tell anyone," I promised. I felt fairly safe, since I'd seen every book in Ida Mae's collection. In fact, quite a few of them had been donated by my mother. I was confident the elderly woman didn't have some kind of secret book collection hidden away somewhere with what is commonly referred to as "titles for those with discriminating tastes." I'd seen some of those titles. It didn't take any discrimination to open the covers. A waste of paper, ink, and thought, in my opinion.

Gabe and Adam came out of the house and started toward us. Ida Mae lowered her voice and took my hand. "He came in to buy a Bible, Hilde. He also asked for a book that would help him understand it. I gave him a commentary I thought would help him." She peered up at me, her dark brown eyes squinting against the sun. "I don't think he's looking for a girlfriend, honey. I think he's looking for a Savior."

If she'd told me I'd forgotten to feed Sherlock for a week, I couldn't have felt worse. What an idiot. Here I was, a Christian, claiming to know God, and I'd missed the signs. Derek had just gone through the worst time of his life and was searching for help. I'd managed to think only of myself and insert my ego into the mix. His interest in me was because he knew I was a Christian. Being near his age, he probably thought I was someone he could talk to, someone who would understand him. Great job I'd done so far. I looked over toward the boardinghouse. Derek was working with Minnie to clean up the yard. Now that I thought about it, he really had changed quite a bit since getting out of jail. He was quieter and seemed more than willing to help out around the house without Mrs. Hudson's constant prodding.

Gabe and Adam finally reached us. Adam had two shoe boxes in his hands and he held them out to Ida Mae. She put them in her lap and opened one of them, shifting through the papers. Gabe and Adam waited expectantly. I knew they were hoping she had insurance. I did, too. But at that moment, all I could really think about was Derek and how I'd let him down. I made up my mind to do something about it as soon as I could.

"Here," she said finally, holding up an envelope. "This is the last thing I got from the insurance company."

Gabe took the envelope and pulled out the letter inside. I moved up next to him so I could see it. It was a policy cancellation notice, dated almost two years ago. I couldn't hold back a sigh of disappointment.

He shook his head and handed it back to Ida Mae. "This means you have no insurance, Ida Mae."

She took the envelope back and placed it in the box. "I'm not a stupid woman, you know," she said carefully. "William always took care of the bills and the insurance. When he died, I was left with some things I didn't understand. I should have gone to someone—asked for help—but I didn't want to be a bother. And in some ways, I just didn't care. When that notice arrived, I looked at it, but I guess I thought it was automobile insurance. Since I'd quit driving and sold my car, I figured there wasn't any need to worry about it. I see I've done a very foolish thing."

Although Ida Mae had always been a strong person, she sounded defeated. I tried to think of something comforting to say, but I needn't have bothered. Before I could get a word out, Mrs. Hudson, who had joined us again after sorting through the broken remnants of her lawn ornaments, spoke up.

"Ida Mae, we'll all see this through together. Eden might

be small, but we're family. My goodness, most people don't even know we exist. I expect God put us all together for a reason. Until that roof is repaired, you're staying with me. I have an empty room, and you'll be comfortable there. After we get you settled, we'll figure out what to do next."

Ida Mae's look of gratitude touched my heart. I wanted to hug Mrs. Hudson until the buttons popped off her calico jumper.

"I know some guys who will work on your roof," Adam said. "I'll bet I can have them out here today to cover the house. At least it will protect your belongings until we can determine everything that needs to be done."

"Oh my goodness," the elderly woman said. "I can't thank you all enough. You really are heaven-sent. God's angels, that's what you are."

At that moment I was feeling more like one of God's fallen angels. "I'm going to check on Sherlock," I said to the small group gathered around Ida Mae. "I'll be right back."

"Hilde, will you ask Derek to get some boxes from the basement?" Mrs. Hudson said. "We can use them to pack up Ida Mae's things."

I smiled. "I'd be happy to." And I was. It gave me the perfect chance to talk to him. As Adam tried to reach one of his clown friends on his cell phone, I took off across the street to talk to Derek. Even though two of Adam's group were gone, there were still well over fifteen men who still belonged to Clowns for Christ. A couple of them were contractors, and one owned a large home improvement store. Ida Mae was in good hands.

I hadn't lied about Sherlock. I really did want to make sure he was okay. Had the storm frightened him? I had no idea how tornadoes affect goldfish. Once when Mrs. Hudson's old tabby cat, Murgatroyd, slipped into my room while the door was open and hopped up on the table where Sherlock's bowl sat, his reaction had been to swim in circles until I grabbed the old cat and put him in the hallway. Sherlock had settled down pretty quickly, but I knew he'd been concerned. Hopefully, the noise from the passing storm hadn't caused a similar reaction.

As I trudged through the sodden yard, trying to step around pieces of debris, I thought I saw something familiar lying near an old oak tree whose limbs had been stripped and broken. Sure enough, it was Gabe's ancient sign, twisted and bent. It had been hanging by a lick and a prayer anyway. It was surely done for now. You could barely make out the name: Bashevis Antiques. I picked it up and carried it with me. For some reason, I couldn't leave it lying on the ground like a piece of discarded trash.

Our dirt road had turned into a mud road. My shoes were definitely a lost cause now, but compared to Ida Mae's loss, mine was nothing.

As I approached the boardinghouse, Derek saw me and turned to go inside. I yelled out his name. The first time he ignored me. The second time he stopped and waited at the top of the stairs, his arms folded across his chest, a scowl on his face. I couldn't blame him. I whispered a prayer for help—and forgiveness. I put Gabe's sign down on the ground and jogged toward Derek, determined to set things right. Minnie stopped her work and watched us.

"Hey, Derek," I called out. "Your aunt sent me over. She wants you to get some boxes from the basement for Ida Mae. I guess she'll be staying here for a while, until her house is repaired."

Minnie stepped up closer. "Did you say Ida Mae was coming to stay?"

I nodded at her, wishing she'd mind her own business for once. Minnie Abercrombie stuck her nose into everything. Nothing happened in our house that Minnie didn't know about.

"That's just like Arabella," she sighed. "Opening up her house to the downtrodden."

"I wouldn't call Ida Mae downtrodden," I said. "She just needs a little help."

"You know what I mean," she snapped. "That house of hers has needed a coat of paint for years, and don't get me started on that awful sign in her window. And selling those old books out of her living room? Well, I mean—"

"About those boxes," I said rather loudly to Derek, cutting Minnie off before she said something that took my focus off mending my fences with Derek. What I might say to Minnie had the potential to be a lot more volatile than my earlier rudeness to Derek.

"I'll take care of it." Derek's voice still held a note of hostility, but I saw a small smile flit across his face before he turned toward the front door. Stopping Minnie before she made any further stupid comments had racked up a small victory for my side.

"Let me help you," I said, bounding up the stairs. He didn't answer, but at least he didn't say no. I followed him down the hall to the basement door.

"I can get the boxes by myself," he said.

I smiled at him. "Why don't you round them up? I want to check on Sherlock, but I'll come back and help you carry them up the stairs. I know they're not heavy, but I'm sure they're a little awkward."

He didn't return my smile. Instead he just shrugged his shoulders and said, "Whatever."

At least he was talking to me. It was better than I deserved. "Okay." I reached out and touched his arm, and then I turned to go to my apartment.

"Hilde," he said in a soft voice, "I didn't mean to upset you out there. I. . ."

"Derek," I said, turning around to face him. "I'm so sorry. I was a little unnerved by the storm. My reaction was totally inappropriate. All I can do is ask you to forgive me."

The edginess he'd carried with him since the incident outside vanished, and he smiled. "That's okay. I understand. I shouldn't have taken it personally. Since all that stuff happened a few months ago. . ." He looked down and his voice grew quieter. "I'm pretty embarrassed about it. I wouldn't blame people if they don't trust me."

"It might take a little while for you to earn back their confidence. I'm sure you can do it."

"Thanks," he said, flashing me one of his million-dollar smiles. "And thanks for offering to help with the boxes. I really can carry them myself, but you can check with me after you make sure your goldfish is okay."

"All right."

"And Hilde," he said, coloring slightly. "There's. . .there's something I'd like to talk to you about sometime if you don't mind. Maybe if you have a few minutes after things settle down. . ."

"Of course. Anytime that's convenient for you."

He nodded and went down the stairs. I hurried to my apartment, thanking God for helping me to mend the damage caused by my selfishness. When I opened the door to my room, everything looked just as I'd left it. I ran over to Sherlock's tank. The big goldfish swam up next to the side and wiggled his fin at me. He seemed fine. Of course, it's a little difficult to figure out just how a goldfish is feeling, so after talking to him for a few minutes, I decided he must be okay. At least he wasn't swimming in circles.

I put a little food in his water and looked out my front windows. Butch and PeeWee had arrived and were starting to move the debris into piles. Adam was off the phone and was helping them while Gabe stood next to Ida Mae. I looked for Mrs. Hudson, but I didn't see her. Her words about being family had touched my heart. In many ways, she was a mother figure to everyone in the house. She certainly wasn't a perfect mother, but she tried. That was enough.

As my phone started to ring, I realized that my own mother may have been watching the weather and heard about the tornado. I chided myself for not calling her sooner. I checked my caller ID. Sure enough, it was Mom.

I answered the phone but barely got "Hello?" out before my mother cut me off.

"Hilde, are you all right? One of the other doctors just told me there was a tornado near Eden."

"I'm fine, Mom. And yes, it came through here. Mrs. Hudson's is fine, but Ida Mae's house lost its roof."

"Oh my goodness, Hilde," she said, her voice trembling. "Living out in the sticks like that. You're just asking for trouble."

My mother's constant attempts to get me to move back to the city had just taken an odd turn. "Mother, are you trying to tell me you think there are tornadoes on the lookout for people who don't live in big cities? Are you serious?"

"Hildegard Bernadette Higgins. Everyone knows they stay away from larger cities because the air is so much hotter."

"Well, I agree there's more hot air in Wichita than in Eden," I said dryly, "but tornadoes hit big cities, too."

She started to say something else, but unless I wanted to

get into a heated debate about where tornadoes were most likely to occur, I had to change tactics.

"Listen, Mother," I said as she began launching into a list of past weather-related tragedies in rural areas, "I have to go. Ida Mae is going to be staying at Mrs. Hudson's for a while. I need to help her move."

Bringing up my elderly neighbor's name did the trick. Mom's focus changed from tornadoes that were intent on my personal destruction to Ida Mae's situation.

"You said she lost her roof?" Mom said. "Her home-owner's insurance should cover that."

I sighed. "If she had some, it would. Unfortunately, she let it lapse after her husband died."

"Oh dear." The distress in her voice was real. My mother had real affection for Ida Mae. They hadn't spent a lot of time together, but their similar love of books had forged a friendship.

"Adam thinks his group will be able to cover the roof until repairs are made. I'm sure they'll do what they can to see the project through."

"Hilde, you have Adam call me, okay? I'll help with the cost."

Sometimes my mother drove me to distraction. And sometimes, like now, I wouldn't trade her for any other mother in the whole world.

"Thanks, Mom. I'll tell him. I'd better get going."

There was a rather long pause on the other end of the phone.

"Mother?"

She cleared her throat. Uh-oh. Whenever my mother clears her throat, what comes next is never good.

"Hilde, something has happened. I want to talk to you about it, but this may not be a good time. Can you meet me for lunch tomorrow?"

So far today, I'd discovered a clown corpse in a grave, I'd been informed my boyfriend was under suspicion of murder, I'd spent time down at the police station, and I'd been through a tornado. A rather busy day in anyone's book. But my mother's statement, "Something has happened," and the fact that she needed to talk to me about it concerned me more than the rest of the day's events.

"I—I suppose I can see you for lunch. I have an appointment at ten thirty. I should be done around noon." I could feel beads of sweat popping out on my forehead along my hairline. "What's this about?"

"Oh, nothing," she said, trying too hard to sound nonchalant. "I'll tell you tomorrow."

Since my appointment was at Willowbrook Funeral Home, Mom picked a restaurant not too far from there. After agreeing to meet her, I hung up the phone. What now? The last time she said, "Something has happened," she'd told me my grandmother had died. Of course, the worst time was when she told me that my father had taken off with his tax attorney. That happened when I was a child, but I still remember it like it was yesterday. In between my father's disappearance and my grandmother's death, there had been a few other heart-to-heart talks that had begun with that much-hated phrase, but right now, I couldn't recall just what they were. Probably some kind of emotional block caused by extreme mental duress. Whatever this was wouldn't be good. This was Mother's way of delivering bad news. Letting the tension build up was part of the fun.

I attempted to shake off the feeling of dread that tried to overtake me. Even though I wasn't hopeful Mom wanted to tell me that she'd decided to quit asking me to get the purple streak taken out of my hair or that she had decided to enthusiastically embrace my career choice, worrying about something that hadn't happened yet was a waste of time. And right now I had enough to think about. One of the biggest problems circulating through my mind was my problem with Adam. I wanted to trust him. I wanted to believe him when he said he had nothing to do with Harold's death.

I sat on the window seat and watched him work side by side with Butch and PeeWee. After a few minutes I got up, said good-bye to Sherlock, and went downstairs to see if I could help Derek.

The rest of the day I tried to think about other things, but the truth kept forcing its way into my conscious mind and wouldn't be denied.

When it came right down to it, I didn't completely trust Adam Sawyer—the man I was falling in love with.

CHAPTER SIX

Tuesday morning, I rolled out of bed tired and sore. Cleaning up the debris and helping Ida Mae move into the vacant room on the second floor had worn me out. Thinking about Adam had added its own stress. Perhaps it was more emotional than physical, but the end result was about the same.

I carried my clothes and toiletries to the bathroom in the hall outside my room. Just getting ready for a shower seemed like a chore. Once I stood under the hot water, I didn't want to move. It felt so good and helped to relax my tight, strained muscles. By the time I got out, I felt a little better, but I was still confused about Adam. We hadn't talked much after the tornado. Not that there was time. Several of his friends had come out to help Ida Mae. They were able to get the top of her house covered with plastic tarps. At least it would be protected from the rain. Barney Bancroft, whose clown name was "B.B.," worked in property insurance. He talked to Ida Mae about getting a new, low-cost policy. He was able to find a roofing company that offered to do the work for a discounted fee if Terry Nicholson, whose clown name was "BoBo," would give them the roofing supplies. A call to my mother took care of the roofing company and the supplies, which Terry gave them at cost.

The men from Clowns for Christ were a godsend. They swooped in, worked hard, tackled problems, and solved them. By the time they left, Eden almost looked like Eden again, and Ida Mae was on her way to getting her home repaired. Although I'd met all the men in the group at one time or another, some I knew better than others. Losing two of their members had certainly taken its toll. It was evident in their overall demeanor. What disturbed me even more than their obvious grief were the looks they kept shooting toward Adam. Although he pretended not to notice, I could tell he was aware of their scrutiny. A little voice in my head asked how I could trust him if the men he'd known and volunteered with for so long were suspicious about Harold's death, too.

I got dressed, fed Sherlock, and then headed for Willowbrook. Before I walked out the front door, I checked the kitchen. Mrs. Hudson was serving Ida Mae her breakfast, and the two were talking like a couple of magpies. Minnie, who was used to being the center of Mrs. Hudson's attention, didn't look too pleased about being second banana. She sat with her arms folded across her ample chest, her sharp nose tilted slightly in the air like she was sniffing out a smell she didn't like. With her dyed red hair and overly made-up eyes, she reminded me of an out-of-sorts clown. And clowns were the last thing I wanted to think about today. I skipped saying "hello" and scooted out the front door before they saw me.

Even though it was rather early, I found Mrs. Hudson's insurance man outside, staring at the carport. I recognized him from the day before. He'd shown up a couple of hours after she called him, bringing with him a man who estimated the damage and gave her the names of contractors who could begin repairs. At first, Mrs. Hudson was rather distraught over her thousand-dollar deductible, but I happened to be standing nearby when the agent informed her that the deductible would be waived in this case. Her excitement was matched only by my suspicion. I'd seen the agent talking to Gabe a few minutes before the news was delivered. I had a pretty good idea just who had waved that deductible bye-bye. I'd seen this kind of generosity before in Eden. When disaster struck, everyone pitched in to help out a neighbor.

The agent's gaze was directed at the roofless metal poles sticking out of the ground. I'd been introduced to him the day before, but I couldn't remember his name. A photographic memory only works if you can see the information you want to remember. Hearing it doesn't work. Especially in my case. My mind was a complete blank.

"Good morning," I said cheerfully.

"Why, Miss Higgins," he said, looking happy to see me. "How nice to run into you again. I'm just double-checking a few things. Terrible storm yesterday." His eyes seemed huge behind his thick-framed glasses.

"Yes. Yes, it was." Great. The guy remembered my name, and I still couldn't recall his. I wanted to jump in my car and take off before he figured it out, but it seemed rude to just run away. "I—I hope we get a new roof on the carport before the next storm."

His owl eyes swung back toward the missing tin roof. "Well, actually, I think we can do a little better than that. The plan is to build a permanent five-car structure with enclosed sides and back. I think you'll like that more than just four poles with a metal roof attached." He looked toward the house. "Your home's really a unique structure, you know. Victorian, actually. The carport needs to fit in." He gave me a big, Cheshire cat grin.

You could have knocked me over with a feather. "That sounds expensive. I didn't think Mrs. Hudson's insurance would cover something like that."

The odd little man chuckled like I'd just told him an extremely funny joke. "Well, you never know. Sometimes things happen that we don't expect."

I was pretty sure I knew how this thing was happening, but I was just thrilled to have protection for my beloved PT Cruiser. If someone was working behind the scenes, good for him. I knew my mother was helping Ida Mae—and I had a pretty good idea Gabe was behind this improvement, as well as the deductible. He knew how concerned I'd been about my car under that rickety old carport during a bad storm. I was aware Gabe had money. Where it came from was a mystery that was most probably going to stay a mystery—along with everything else about him.

"Well, thanks for all your work," I said as I opened my car door. I was glad I hadn't been put into a situation that would have forced me to come up with his name.

"Miss Higgins," he said before I was able to make a clean getaway. "I do have a quick question."

I pushed back a sigh. "Yes?"

He blinked rapidly a few times and pointed toward Gabe's place across the street. "The man who lives there. I believe he told me his last name was Bashevis. Am I wrong about that?"

"No. That's his name. Why do you ask?"

He frowned. "Oh, nothing. About an hour ago a man drove by here. He was looking for someone, but I didn't know the person he asked about. I told him that, and he left. It sounded similar to Bashevis, but that wasn't it." He shrugged. "I guess maybe he had the wrong town."

It certainly didn't matter, and now I was running even later to my appointment. "Well, okay. Thanks again for everything. I've really got to be going."

Mr. What's-His-Name waved at me and went back to staring at the remnants of our carport. I pulled out before he could think of something else to ask me.

All the way to Willowbrook, I pondered the confusion I felt about Adam. Although I certainly didn't see him as a murderer, the clues pointed right to him. The car, the appointment book, the accusations from Harold. No wonder the police suspected him. The other thing that bothered me was that early morning appointment. Adam had asked me to make sure Harold delivered Marvin's hat because he had an important meeting. Then he told me it was canceled. Convenient. After thinking about it for a few minutes, I pulled into the parking lot of a grocery store and stuck my hand in my purse, looking for my cell phone. I found it after removing my billfold, four grocery receipts, a bag of cough drops, a candy bar I kept in case of a chocolate emergency, that Gaither light, and a pen from "Harry's Happy Hour Hideaway." The pen was going to have to go. Harry's didn't sound like the type of place where I would happily hide away.

I jammed everything back into my purse and punched in the number for Adam's office, knowing he wasn't there. Tammy Sue, the receptionist, answered the phone.

"Harris, Pringle, and Sanders," she said lightly.

"Hi, Tammy Sue," I said, trying to sound nonchalant. "Is Adam in?"

"Hi, Hilde. No, he took the day off. You didn't know?"

I hesitated. "Oh, that's right. Sorry. I've been getting a little confused lately. It's probably all the stress of the last few days. You know, I was sure Adam told me he had an appointment yesterday morning. I guess I got that wrong, too."

"Yesterday morning?" she repeated. "No, he didn't have anything scheduled. He called at six thirty and left a message saying he would be in late." She sighed. "It's understandable that you're confused, Hilde. Things have been really hectic lately. James and his wife are on a cruise, and Bucky is recovering from gallstone surgery. We've had a lot of concerned clients because of the stock market swings lately. Of course, Bucky can't help being out, but I sure wish James had put off his trip for a while."

James was James Sanders, one of the managing partners of Harris, Pringle, and Sanders. Bucky was Clarence Pringle. But their vacation and surgery situations didn't interest me. The news that Adam didn't have an appointment was the only thing I could think about. I commiserated with Tammy Sue for a couple of minutes, and then I hung up.

I stared at the people coming in and out of the grocery store, feeling bewildered. Adam had lied to me about the appointment. He'd called in around six thirty, thirty minutes before the meeting written in Harold's appointment book.

I finally forced myself to start the car and drive to Willowbrook, but my mind was seized with trepidation. Wasn't there only one reason Adam would tell me he had an appointment he didn't really have? He was trying to cover up something. Could it possibly be Harold's murder?

CHAPTER SEVEN

I work in a funeral home, but you're the one who looks like you've seen a ghost," Paula said as she led me back to my newest client. "What's wrong with you?"

I shook my head. "I really don't want to talk about it right now."

"I know what that means. You're so bugged you can't even put it into words. Not good." She turned around to stare at me. "Your mother?"

I shook my head. "No. That's next. I'm meeting her for lunch. 'Something has happened.'"

"Uh-oh." Paula was aware of my mother's propensity for dropping emotional bombs. "So the day after finding a dead clown in a grave and being hauled down to the big house, your mother has another one of her mind-numbing announcements."

"I haven't even told you about the tornado," I said glumly.

Paula stopped in her tracks and faced me. "I heard about a tornado, but I had no idea it was anywhere near you. Are you okay? Everyone in Eden okay?"

I briefly recounted the storm and its aftermath.

"Wow, Hilde. If you drank, I'd suggest we drop everything and spend the afternoon at the Nomad."

"Well, thanks, but I don't think alcohol would help me right now." I didn't want to offend Paula, but I didn't care for the Nomad anyway. She'd dragged me there a couple of times. They have great cappuccino, but the atmosphere just isn't for me. Lots of single people on the prowl for other single people. With booze. Not a good combination.

Paula reached out and put her hand on my shoulder. "Okay then, why don't you come back here this evening, and we'll go out for a quiet dinner. Someplace where we can talk. My treat."

I started to say no, but then I realized spending the evening with Paula would give me a way out of seeing Adam tonight. And I needed a little time to process everything. "You know what? That sounds good. What time do you get off?"

"I should be ready to go by five thirty. Just wait in the parking lot, and we'll drive to the restaurant together. How about DeFazio's?"

"Wow. I could really go for their sausage manicotti topped off by one of those incredible cream puffs. But why don't we split it?"

Paula smiled. "Quit treating me like the poor relative. I make more money than you do."

And I had fewer bills than she did, but the last thing I wanted to do was offend her. "Okay. You know, it sounds perfect. Just what I need."

"By the way, the Martinez funeral has been moved to Thursday morning at ten."

I cleared my throat. "Will he. . .will he. . ."

"Is he okay?" Paula said with a grin. "Yes, he's fine. No problems. We have the casket locked down to prevent all that clown makeup from drying out. You won't need to do any touch-up."

I breathed a sigh of relief. Although one of Marvin's "clown brothers" had guided me through the process, I'd been asked to apply his makeup and supervise the placing of his costume. You'd think I'd be over my fear of clowns, since I was actually dating one, but there were still some remnants of "icky" that clung to my psyche. A serious illness as a child had brought me into contact with clowns who entertained at a hospital where I spent a great deal of time. Somehow, I'd associated all clowns with that experience, and my revulsion had grown until it was out of control. Being forced to confront them through Adam and his friends had helped—a lot. But I still thought most clown makeup was a little horrifying. And watching the Stephen King movie *It* when I was a teen had certainly not helped. I'd had nightmares for years after that silly thing.

Paula led me into a back room reserved for those who no longer had concerns in this life—not even scary clowns. Waiting for me was Tabitha Vanderkellen. Mrs. Vanderkellen had been an important person in Wichita. Born into old money and long-standing prestige, she'd risen above her titles and public persona by becoming one of the most generous and warmhearted citizens ever to grace the streets of the city. Comfortable in the halls of the super rich and even more at home serving at soup kitchens and missions, she'd lived her Christian faith with incredible grace and compassion. She was proof that owning money didn't necessarily mean money had to own you.

Paula handed me a picture of Mrs. Vanderkellen that had been taken at a recent charity event. Her eyes sparkled with intelligence and humor.

"We're having the service at Central Christian Church. She was a member of a smaller church, but there are so many people who want to attend, Central opened its doors to help."

I hoped Central Christian's large sanctuary was big enough to contain all the people touched by Mrs. Vanderkellen. "What a great way to live your life," I said as I began to remove the brushes from my bag.

"Yes. Yes, it is," Paula agreed. "Well, I'm off to an appointment with the daughter of a man who was so selfish the whole family is glad to be rid of him." She sighed. "Night-and-day family interviews, I can tell you that."

Paula turned to go as I began brushing the elderly woman's soft, white hair. It was already clean. Mortuaries always wash bodies when they come in. It rids the corpse of any lingering germs and body fluids. About an hour later, I put my curling iron, hair spray, and combs back into my satchel.

Mrs. Vanderkellen's hair looked lovely—just like the photo. I pulled my camera from my purse and took a few pictures. It wasn't really necessary at Willowbrook, but it had become second nature. It was a habit I'd begun a few months after I started working with the dearly departed. Someone from one of the homes had made the decision to change one of my hairstyles. The family hated the end result and blamed me. Now I keep proof of my work for a few days after each case. Following the funeral and the burial, I delete the pictures, making sure no one else sees them.

After I packed all my supplies, I completed my work with Mrs. Vanderkellen by praying for her family and thanking God for the opportunity to work with her. After saying "Amen," I checked my watch. Drat. I was running a bit behind. My mother hates tardiness, but it seems like every time we make arrangements to meet, I'm always late. I grabbed my stuff and made a beeline for the front entrance. Paula's office door was closed, so I didn't stop to say good-bye.

Even though I hurried as fast as I could, I arrived about five minutes late to Mom's favorite new restaurant, Mission. Not the Mission. Just Mission. And God help you if you accidentally stick "the" on the front. I always thought it was just a word, but in the world of the *trés chic*, "the" seems to be the poor cousin second removed from all other words that have style and prominence. Uttering it combined with "Mission" was so frowned upon, I made sure I did it frequently. It caused my mother undue emotional stress. Shame on me for finding it funny.

Anyway, I pulled my PT into the parking lot just in time to snatch the last spot near the door. A man in a Cadillac shot me a disapproving look. I wasn't sure if it was because he wanted my space or because he didn't feel my car belonged among the Beemers, Caddies, and Lexuses that filled the other slots. Since I wouldn't trade my PT for any car in the lot, it didn't bother me even a smidgen. I just smiled, waved, and traipsed into the restaurant.

I had on my "good" clothes, since I'd just come from a job. Usually, I'd have on my leather boots, jeans, and a T-shirt. Not sure how I would have been welcomed into Mission, since almost everyone there was dressed in suits and ties. Of course, the really, really rich don't care. They wear whatever they want, and no one looks askance at them. But since I wasn't toting the latest purse that cost more than what I make in a year, I definitely got the once-over from the hostess, who was obviously expecting someone else when I opened the door. Her face fell so far I was surprised she didn't have to reach down and scrape it up from the floor.

"May I help you?" she intoned through her nasal cavities.

For just a second, I thought about asking her if this was Oliver's Burgers and Bait, but I squelched the temptation. "I'm here to meet Dr. Naomi Higgins."

The sun came out again. "Why, yes. Dr. Higgins is already here. Let me show you to her table."

I followed her through the entrance into the restaurant itself. Since this was my first time to actually darken the doors of my mother's new hangout, I wasn't quite certain what to expect. It was almost exactly what I'd imagined. Minimalism had nothing on Mission. White walls highlighted with brushed metal pillars and lights. No pictures on the walls—just strange long strands of beadlike ropes hanging in clumps. The tables were black, square, and plain. And the white leather seats looked like gussied-up lawn chairs.

My mother waited at a table smack in the middle of the dining room. I liked to sit in the corner, where conversation was easier and other diners not so visible. But Mom had no problem being the center of attention. It wasn't that she craved it. She just belonged there, and she knew it. As usual, she was dressed to the nines. She wore a black designer pantsuit that highlighted her blond hair and lithe body. When she got back to the hospital, she would change the jacket for a white lab coat—and she'd still look coordinated. I glanced down at my black slacks, which, when compared to my mother's pants, appeared decidedly washed out. My shoes were department store specials—and looked it. In the restaurant lighting, I could make out the wrinkles in my cream-colored blouse. Funny how I hadn't noticed them before. I was somewhat comforted to notice that quite a few other Mission patrons appeared rather shabby compared to Mother.

"You're late again, Hilde," she said as I approached the table. She sighed deeply and handed me a menu as I sat down. "I've already ordered."

"Thanks for waiting, Mom."

"I don't have time to sit here all day. I've spoken to you before about promptness. People trust prompt people."

"They also trust people who don't leave their dead mother's hair half done." I tried to say it lightly, but it still sounded petulant. Oh well, that's me. The petulant daughter with the wrinkled blouse and the purple streak in her hair. Might as well stay true to form.

"Hildegard," my mother hissed, looking around her. "Let's leave that out of it if you don't mind." Her frown turned into the rather fake-looking smile her patients probably saw when they woke up from brain surgery. "We've been getting along so well lately, let's not tear down what we've built up with snippy comments, okay?"

This was one of those *Twilight Zone* moments, when I could swear I heard the popular theme from that long-gone series playing in my head. I wanted to stand up and say, "Are you actually serious? Do you ever listen to yourself? What about your promptness soliloquy? Was that designed to promote mother/daughter harmony?"

But of course, I didn't say it. It wouldn't do any good. My mother's ear was tuned in to my shortcomings. She rarely recognized her own. However, for the last several months, we really had been doing a lot better. Getting upset because of my mother's admonition wasn't worth losing what we'd gained.

"I'm sorry, Mother," I said as meekly as I could. "You're right. Please forgive me for being late—and for being snippy. Yesterday's events have left me a little worse for wear."

Our waitress came to the table to take my order. While I quickly looked through the menu, I realized she looked more like my mother than I did. In fact, their blond hair matched so closely, I wanted to ask the number on their hair dye bottle. Not that my mother would be caught dead using hair dye. Unfortunately, while my mother's more authentic child stared at me disapprovingly, I realized the entire menu was in French. Not wanting to embarrass myself further, I reeled off, "I'll have the *compote de joue de boeuf.*" At least I recognized the word *beef* when I saw it. My time with Monsieur Max had finally paid off. I was fairly confident that my pronunciation had been spot on, too. Even my long-lost sister seemed impressed. She thanked me, grabbed the menu, and sashayed away. Feeling a little more confident, I gave my mother a self-satisfied smile.

"Good job, Hilde," she said, one eyebrow raised in amusement. "I had no idea you were partial to beef cheek."

It took everything inside me to keep my smile in place. "There are many things about me you don't know, Mother."

She picked up her glass of sparkling water. "Yes, I'm sure that's true, dear. I guess if you're partial to that canned meat you devour all the time, you can also be happy with meat from inside a cow's mouth."

"Funny, you had nothing but nice things to say about my

meat loaf," I shot back, hoping to divert our attention from spitty cow cheek. My mother had attended a dinner where my meat loaf was the main course. Silly woman assumed I'd used some kind of hamburger in the recipe. She complimented me on it more than once—in public.

"You shouldn't have tried to deceive me like that," she said, sniffing. "People should know what they're eating."

"You mean, I should have told you I'd made the meat loaf from SPAM? The same way you could have told me I'd just ordered something made with bovine mouth?"

My mother's right eyebrow shot up again. It certainly was getting a workout today. "I thought you said you knew what you'd ordered." Her voice held a hint of triumph.

I looked around to see if anyone else had heard my mother's revelation that her daughter was an uncivilized lout who ordered food based on ego instead of intelligence. But no one was the least bit interested in us. "I didn't say any such thing. I simply said you don't know everything about me."

This time her smile was genuine. "Well, at least I know what beef cheek is."

"Okay, you've got me, Mom. I'm an idiot. I had no idea what I was ordering. I guess now I'm going to have to pay the piper."

She laughed. "Actually, beef cheek tastes rather like tender shredded beef. You won't hate it."

Just what I wanted to hear. "You won't hate your food" is

the kind of recommendation all diners crave. With a sigh, I took a drink of water and then set my glass down.

"Okay, Mom. Now what is it that you have to tell me? Exactly what has happened?"

She tapped her perfectly filed fingers on the edge of her coffee cup. "I—I don't quite know how to tell you this, Hilde," she said. "I'm afraid you will be somewhat shocked."

A quick mental run-through of my remaining relatives didn't yield any names that would cause me severe trauma due to their passing. Unless my mother had decided to leave the medical profession and become a nun, I couldn't come up with anything that would throw me into counseling. Nevertheless, my stomach was so tight, I wasn't sure I could force down a single bite of compote de joue de boeuf. Of course, when it comes to my mother, she's always managed to go above and beyond telling me things I don't expect to hear. This turned out to be right up there with "It's time you found out that you're adopted," although that might actually be *good* news.

"Hildegard, I've heard from your father."

I stared at her. I knew what the words meant; they just didn't make any sense. "I'm sorry, Mother. I don't understand. It sounded like you said you've heard from my father."

She opened her mouth to say something else, but just then our waitress stepped up to check on our water consumption. After filling our glasses to the top, she wisely departed. It might have been the deafening silence that clued her in to the emotionally charged atmosphere at our table or the fact that all the color had probably left my face. Whatever it was, she scooted away pretty fast, leaving me with my mouth hanging open.

"For goodness' sakes, Hilde," my mother said in a low voice. "It's not like I just told you we're from another planet."

"Funny, Mom," I said wryly. "Although that would explain a lot." My mind worked frantically to process my mother's revelation, but the sound of grinding and the feeling that smoke might start pouring out my ears at any moment signaled it wasn't happening. "I guess I thought. . .I don't know. . .that after more than fifteen years, he was. . .he was. . ."

"Dead?" Mom shook her head. "That's probably my fault. After your father left, I wouldn't allow you to talk about him. In my mind, he was dead." She gave me a tremulous smile. "I guess you can add this to the list of things I haven't dealt with correctly. Just one more thing that has impeded your emotional health."

Emotional health? What emotional health? "Well, it would have been nice if we could have talked about it a little. I mean, one day he's my daddy, and the next day he's 'that creep who ran out with his tax attorney.' For a while, I thought he'd come back—or at least call me. Then after a few years, I just quit thinking about him altogether. Much easier on the heart."

"Yes, it was easier, but now I wonder if it was right." My

mother was starting to say something else when our waitress brought our food. Mother had some kind of salad with chicken and artichokes. My compote de joue de boeuf was a square piece of meat stuffed with several other ingredients. Except for the pistachios, it looked oddly like a slice of SPAM. Except it didn't smell quite as yummy. Positioned next to the square of boeuf was a glob that looked like mustard with seeds in it. There were two small pickles, three pearl onions, and something that looked like grass. And that was it. Good thing I wasn't hungry. Also a good thing my mom was picking up the tab. Forty dollars for a slab of cow's cheek was a bit much—especially if it could be consumed in two bites. The waitress walked away after assuring herself that we were properly appreciative of the chance to sample their food—sample being the key word.

After bowing my head and saying a short prayer, which my mother pretended not to notice, "Where has he been?" popped out of my mouth as I picked up my fork. Funny how "What did he want?" didn't come out first.

"He's been living in Hawaii all this time. He runs his own real estate company."

"Real estate? I thought he was a mortgage broker."

"He was." My mother stabbed a piece of her salad with her fork. "He hated it, Hilde. He worked long hours and felt tied down. I can still remember how unhappy he was."

I cut off a piece of forty-dollar beef face with my fork and moved on to question two on the hit parade. "So what does he want?" With a gulp, I stuck my fork in my mouth. Hmmm. Not bad. But not as good as SPAM.

Mother chewed slowly, allowing me to stew in my own jowl juice. It didn't help my digestion, which was already asking what in the world I'd just jammed into it. My stomach gurgled as it tried to figure out what to do with something brand new—and strange.

Finally, she put her fork down. "He wants to see you, Hilde. He's coming to Wichita."

My stomach finally decided its course. I almost didn't make it to the little mademoiselle's room in time.

CHAPTER ▌▌▌ EIGHT

After ridding myself of my run-in with beef mouth, I left the restaurant promising my mother I'd think about seeing my father. And I did. For about ten seconds. My answer was a resounding "no." As a Christian, I knew I had no choice but to forgive him—and to the best of my ability, I had. I mean, I didn't want him dead or covered with warts. But seeing him again after all these years was really asking too much. I'd waited most of my life hoping to hear something from him, but in all that time there was never so much as a "Hello, I'm alive. Are you?" Why should I help him ease his conscience now? No thanks. I called my mother on her cell phone and told her to tell my father I wasn't interested. Although she didn't admit it, she sounded relieved.

I was only about three blocks from the restaurant when my cell rang. It was Sweet Slumberland Funeral Home. Did I have time to fix a problem with a client whose viewing was about two hours from now? I told them I'd be there in twenty minutes and turned around. Emergency fixes aren't all that unusual in my business. Most funeral home cosmeticians do great work when preparing the body, but because they're not trained hairstylists, sometimes they need someone like me to step in. Most of my regulars call me whenever they have a female client. Some of my semi-regulars call me when things go wrong, like today. Although the majority of my clients are women, I've worked with a few men. Several of those situations involved styling a hairpiece. It actually takes some effort to make one look right. Placing a hairpiece incorrectly can give the impression that a raccoon wandered in and passed away on top of the departed's head. Not a good look for anyone—especially a corpse.

I spent the next hour combing out a well-meaning employee's attempt at an upswept style with curls. When I finished, the grateful funeral director paid me my usual fee plus a fifty-dollar tip. I left feeling good about my work and thankful for the chance to get the situation with my mother and father off my mind for a while.

I drove back toward Willowbrook but stopped in for awhile at Starbucks to think about my father. As I lingered over a cinnamon dolce latte, I tried to pull up some memory of my dad besides the last time I saw him, driving away in his girlfriend's bright orange sports car—not even bothering to look back and wave good-bye. A few months ago, in a rare moment of complete honesty in our relationship, my mother had finally explained my hatred toward all things orange. Although her explanation had helped me regain my enjoyment of citrus fruit, I guess it hadn't erased the pain still crouching inside me. For the first time, it occurred to me that if my father's sudden reappearance was difficult for me, it had to be even harder for my mother. She appeared calm and collected. Of course, that was par for the course with Mom. Very few things rattled her, but the betrayal I felt from my dad must pale in comparison to what she'd gone through. I could still remember the fear and worry on her face as she struggled to take care of us alone. But she'd found a way. She moved her mother into our house so there would always be someone for me to come home to. Then she went back to work as a nurse and put herself through medical school. For several years, I hardly ever saw her. Eventually things got better. When I was thirteen, we moved to a nicer house. Then my grandmother, who'd not been well for quite some time, went into an assisted living facility. Finally, I moved out. Not long after that, Mom's career really took off. She sold our house and bought the monstrosity she lives in now. Money certainly isn't a problem anymore. From the outside, her life looks perfect. But in all these years, she's never remarried. In fact, as far as I know, she's only dated a couple of men. And neither one of them stayed around for very long. I have my own baggage because of my father's abandonment, but my mother has packed some of her own as well. A fear of men appears to be at the top of the list.

My attempt to bring back memories of my dad was unsuccessful. Even my photographic memory didn't have the power to dredge them up. I could see someone reading books to me. I knew it was my father, but I couldn't see him clearly. As I sipped my latte, I realized there was very little left in my conscious mind about the man whose DNA I shared. Meeting him didn't really matter that much. He was a man I didn't know. And for the life of me, I couldn't find any reason to get to know him now. By the time I was ready to meet Paula, I was as sure as I could be that my decision not to see him was the right one. It certainly wasn't my job to help him clear his conscience. Nor was I under any obligation to mend fences he'd broken himself.

I felt pretty good as I drove to Willowbrook. Anyway, my mind was clear, but my stomach still gurgled. Stupid beef cheeks.

I pulled up in the parking lot around five fifteen. A little after five thirty, Paula came out and jogged over to my car.

"Are you driving?" she asked when she opened the passenger door.

"Might as well," I said with a smile.

She climbed in without an argument. Paula's car was always a mess. I hated trying to find a place to put my feet between the empty water bottles and food wrappers that littered the floor. The car seat itself was always an adventure, too. There were usually stains that didn't bode well for my derrière.

"So what did your mom want to talk to you about?" she asked as she fastened her seat belt.

On the way to the restaurant, I recounted the events at

lunch. Paula's mouth hung open in amazement throughout most of our journey. My mother's warning about "closing your mouth so you won't catch a fly" popped into my head several times. Fortunately, we arrived at DeFazio's fly free.

The warm, rich tones and simple elegance of one of Wichita's best restaurants created an atmosphere of relaxation and anticipation. Mission, on the other hand, made me feel as if I were going to a job interview for a position about ten pay grades above my capabilities. Paula ordered linguine with pesto. I selected the sausage manicotti. Nothing in French and no beef cheeks anywhere to be found.

After the waitress brought us both a cup of coffee, Paula asked for a more detailed explanation of the events from the past couple of days. As I reeled off one disaster after another, even I had a hard time believing that this much could go wrong in one person's life.

"Whew," she said when I finished. "I hardly know where to start." She wrinkled her nose and stared at me. "I guess my first question is about Adam. Why aren't you with him tonight? I mean, if the man I was in love with was accused of murder, I'd spend every waking moment by his side, supporting him and being there if he needed to talk." Paula's bright green eyes narrowed. "You do believe him, don't you?"

"Of course I do," I said, a little too quickly. I took another sip of coffee while Paula watched me. I set my cup down and frowned at her. "I really don't believe Adam is capable of killing someone, Paula. It's just not in him."

She had just opened her mouth to respond when I saw her glance over my shoulder. Her face registered shock. I turned around to see what had upset her and found myself staring at her parents, headed straight for our table.

"You didn't know your folks were going to be here tonight?" I whispered when I turned around.

She shook her head slowly. "They asked me to have dinner with them, but I told them I couldn't leave the office. Just follow my lead."

I wasn't quite sure what she meant by that, but it didn't sound good. Before I had a chance to question her, Rene and Davis Hilgenfeld stepped up to our table. And they didn't look happy.

"I thought you said you had to work late tonight, Paula," Rene said. She didn't bother to acknowledge my presence.

"I did, Mother," Paula said, looking as guilty as she really was. "But Gus changed his mind at the last minute. Hilde just happened to be at Willowbrook, so we decided to go out for dinner. I knew you were already gone, and I had no idea where you were." She frowned. "What are you doing here? I thought you and Dad hated eating out."

"My boss gave us a gift certificate for our anniversary," Paula's father said, his face screwed up like he'd just digested something that didn't agree with him. Maybe he'd had beef cheeks, too. "We only used it because we didn't want it to go to waste. I must say, though, I wish he'd put his money to better use. We could have prepared five meals at home for the same amount."

Davis is a rather small man. He believes in running his family by a strict set of rules—and exceptions are rarely made. Especially for his daughter. After shooting Paula a look of disapproval—one that I'd seen before—they excused themselves and left. I wanted to stand up and yell, "Nice to see you, too!" But of course, I didn't. More for Paula's sake than theirs. I felt sorry for her, but she wasn't off the hook.

I glared at her. "Okay, let's take this one point at a time. First of all, you lied to your parents. Not cool. And just for your information, if they'd asked me to confirm your little story, I'd have told the truth. Secondly, you blew your parents off on their anniversary? That stinks, Paula."

"Are you finished?"

"No. I know your parents get on your nerves, but they deserve more respect than that. You should be having dinner with them. Not me." I shook my head. "Man, if only I had a mom and a dad who could celebrate their anniversary."

At that moment, the waitress brought our food to the table. It smelled heavenly, but I'd lost my appetite. How could Paula treat her parents like that? After the waitress left, I prayed over my food and took a bite. It was delicious, but I had no interest in it. I felt sick inside.

I looked up to find Paula staring at me with tears in her eyes. "Listen, Hilde. Please don't be mad at me. I'm sorry I lied. I just can't stand to be around them. Things were better when they planned to move away, but after my dad's new job fell through and they had no choice but to stay in Wichita, our relationship got even worse. It's like they blame me for what happened. They disapprove of everything I do. No. . ." She hesitated for a moment. "They disapprove of *me*. Completely. Every second I'm with them I feel like a failure. Can you blame me for running away from that?"

"I'm not really mad at you," I said with a sigh. "Sorry. I don't know why I got so upset. It's just that with my dad showing up out of the blue. . . I don't know. I guess I think anyone with two parents is pretty lucky. Maybe that's not always true." I shook my head. "But I do know what it's like not to be accepted. My mother is always finding something to criticize me for."

Paula dabbed at her eyes with her napkin. "Don't compare our parents. It's different. Very different. Your mom may not always understand some of the things you do, but she's always accepted you. As a person, I mean. That's the difference. You really don't know what it feels like to be a total loser in a parent's eyes. And in my case, the rejection is doubled."

I gazed at my friend, stunned. She was right. I'd never doubted my mother's love. And I knew she wanted the best for me. I also knew she believed in me. She always had. Her desire for me to "live up to my potential," as she liked to say, was the reason she nagged me sometimes. What Paula was trying to tell me was that her parents saw no potential in her at all.

"Paula, I'm so sorry." I reached over and touched her arm.

"Listen. You are beyond a doubt one of the smartest, most talented people I've ever known. Look at how you've moved up at Willowbrook. Gus trusts you completely." Gus Dorado, the owner of Willowbrook Funeral Home, had promoted Paula from secretary and gofer to her current position as a senior funeral director. She oversaw the daily operations of the funeral home with little or no oversight from Gus, who'd been extremely busy with plans to open another location.

"I know he does, and I can't tell you what that means to me. I would never do anything to let him down."

I took another bite of my manicotti. This time it tasted better. "You know, I've told you before that God loves you like a father. I'm starting to realize that I've been saying the wrong thing."

Paula shot me that oh-no-here-we-go-again look.

"Wait a minute. Hear me out. Forget the father reference. We keep comparing God to your father. Let's try this. God loves you like Gus loves you, Paula. When you belong to Him, there's complete acceptance. You never have to work for His love. He never judges you. And He never gives up on you. He's Gus—only a million times better."

Paula laughed and pointed her fork at me. "Okay. Now *that* I can understand. And I like it." She sliced off a piece of her steak but stopped before her fork reached her mouth, setting it back down on her plate. "My parents use their religion as a way to highlight my faults. You use it as a way to offer me hope. It's hard to understand how one religion can produce such different reactions."

"I'm not sure, but I think it has to do with something my pastor says. It's the difference between religion and relationship. Jesus didn't like religion either. Being a Christian isn't adopting a set of rules. It's allowing God to come into your life and. . .I don't know. Make your life mean something, I guess." I grinned at her. "You're not talking to a theologian here. You're talking to someone who loves God—and loves being loved by God."

"I think that's probably the best person in the world to talk to," Paula said softly. "Someone who loves you—and loves God." She sliced off another piece of steak. "I have to admit that no matter what I've tried, there's still an empty place inside me. And my life hasn't really changed. I can talk myself into happiness for a while, but it never lasts."

"If you'll just stop comparing God to your parents, your life would really change. I'm serious."

She looked at me with amusement. "And if you'd ever stop comparing Adam to your dad, your life would really change."

I almost dropped my fork. "I'm not doing that."

Paula sighed. "You always do that, Hilde. Adam isn't the first man you've rejected because you couldn't trust him. You did it in school, and you're doing it now. Granted, this situation is a little different, but I can tell you're starting to doubt him. I saw it in your face during your little speech before my parents showed up." She frowned at me. "I admit that I've been comparing God to my dad, and I guess he's not the best example of fatherhood. But you have to admit that you've been judging men by your father. The question is, Hilde, do you trust Adam? Do you believe in him? If you do, you need to let him know that. And you need to stand by him." She smiled sadly. "I've been with a lot of men, but I've never had anyone like Adam. He's special. And he really loves you. Yet you're so afraid that he might abandon you like your father did, you're planning to abandon him first, just to protect yourself."

There have been few times in my twenty-three years of life when I could say I was actually stunned by something someone said to me. This was definitely one of those moments. Was Paula right? Was I suspicious about Adam's involvement in Harold's murder because I was afraid of being hurt again?

"For crying out loud, Hilde," Paula said. "Say something. You look like I just flushed Sherlock down the toilet."

"I—I think you might be right. Why didn't I see this before?"

Paula arched one of her perfectly shaped eyebrows. "Wait a minute. Are you shocked because of what I said or because I said it? Surely this isn't the first time I've ever been right about something."

Her offended expression made me laugh. "No, this isn't the first time you've been right about something." I reached over and took her hand. "I promise to give this some thought.

I don't want my father's bad decisions to ruin my chance with Adam." I smiled at her. "You're right about him, you know. He is special. Thank you, Paula. For being honest with me."

She squeezed my hand and then pulled her own away. "No problem." She blushed and stared at her plate. "You know, this group I've been hanging around with. . .this New Age group." She shook her head. "After spending time with them, going to their meetings, I convinced myself that I could sense things about people. Read their auras. But I'm beginning to have doubts about the reality of my. . .abilities. There have been times I hit it pretty close. And other times I failed miserably. But understanding your situation didn't have anything to do with spiritual energy or auras. It came from knowing you. From investing time in our relationship."

"Does this mean you'll stop trying to 'read me'?"

Paula nodded. "Yes. I think it does. Maybe I don't have all the answers after all. I have to admit that, except for the few times I talked myself into believing I was happy, my life has been a real mess." She stared at me through narrowed eyes. "Look. Don't get carried away or anything, but maybe I do need to find out a little more about God. It's possible I've been judging Him by my parents. You're a Christian, and you don't treat me like I have horns growing out of my head." She pointed her finger at me. "Don't push me though, okay? I need to do this my own way."

I raised my water glass toward her. "Fair enough. I salute you."

Paula grinned and raised her glass. "I salute you, too." We

clinked our glasses together. "Now what are you going to do about Adam?"

"I'm going to enjoy this great dinner, spend a little more time with my wonderful friend, and then I'm going over to Adam's so I can let him know I intend to stand by him, no matter what happens. Then I'll probably kiss him. More than once."

"Now that sounds like the best idea you've had in ages."

We finished dinner, and I took her back to Willowbrook. I watched as she drove away, thankful that she'd been brave enough to talk to me about Adam. She was right. I'd dated a few guys, but every time they'd tried to move closer, I found something wrong with the relationship. Finally, I just stopped dating. Until Adam. He'd gotten closer to me than any man ever had, and I'd begun to believe I might be falling in love with him. Wondering if he might have killed Harold was probably nothing more than an excuse—a way out. When I really looked into my heart, I knew he couldn't possibly have killed anyone. Adam was one of the most loving, loyal people I'd ever known. There was no possibility he could have taken someone else's life.

I was at a crossroads, and I had to make a decision. Could I really put my trust in a man? Could I love him so much that I could overcome the hurt my father's desertion had caused me? By the time I pulled up in front of Adam's duplex, I was certain the answer was "yes." I glanced at my watch. It was almost eight thirty. I was trying to decide whether or not I should call to let him know I was outside and wanted to see him or if I should just barge in, when his front door opened and a woman stepped out. I couldn't see her very well, but I had no problem seeing what she did. She put her arms around Adam and kissed him, and he certainly didn't push her away.

I threw my car into gear and peeled away.

CHAPTER NINE

"So let me see if I have this right," Gabe said, his thick eyebrows knit together. "After deciding that Adam is the love of your life and that you trust him completely, you see him with another woman and you take off without even talking to him. Is that correct?"

"Don't try to make it sound like I'm the one who did something wrong," I said crossly. I picked up the cup of tea he'd made for me and took a sip. "He had his arms around her, Gabe. There's no way to make that sound innocent."

"And there's no way to trust someone without trusting them. Either you do or you don't."

I shook my head so hard I made myself a little dizzy. "I don't intend to end up like my mother. Not everyone is worthy of trust. My father is a perfect example of that."

Gabe sighed and poured himself another cup of tea. We sat at the table in the kitchen. It had started to rain outside—again. The sound of raindrops on the roof and the low lighting made for a cozy feeling. But my insides weren't feeling cozy. I knew what I'd seen, and no amount of

Gabe's gentle cajoling could change that.

"Have you prayed about this?" he asked.

"Yes. No. I mean, not yet."

"My suggestion is that you get some alone time with God and find out what He thinks. You do trust *Him*, right?"

"Of course I do," I said a little more sharply than I meant to. "I trust you, too. I know you believe in Adam. But why? What makes you so sure he's not cheating on me? Or worse?"

"I'm not sure if you're referring to the incident tonight or the murder. But let's take the murder first. Most importantly, my instincts tell me that Adam couldn't have done it. I've met a lot of people in my life. Some good, some bad. Some very, very bad. After a while you get a sixth sense. Adam is a good man who loves God. I don't believe he would ever take another person's life, especially a friend's. Going beyond my feelings, I look at the facts in a situation. No matter how these supposed clues seem to add up, there is one overwhelming fact that doesn't make sense. Something I can't get around. Has it occurred to you that if Adam had really killed Harold, he would have tried to come up with a better alibi than the one he has? Adam is certainly not a stupid person. In fact, he's one of the sharpest men I've ever known."

"A better alibi? He doesn't have one at all."

"Exactly. This murder wasn't planned. No one in their right mind would kill someone out in the open like that, where almost anyone could see them."

"But Mr. Diggs did see him."

"No, Hilde. Mr. Diggs said he saw a car. He didn't say he saw a person. And he certainly didn't say that he saw Adam. But my point is that when someone plans a murder, they do it behind closed doors. And they usually set it up in a way that will draw suspicion away from them. Not point it right to them."

"So the murder occurred on the spur of the moment," I said. "Something Harold said made Adam angry, and he hit him with a shovel."

"Okay, for the sake of argument, let's assume that's true," Gabe said. He sat back in his chair and folded his arms. "It leads to my second point. If I lost my temper and killed another human being—and I didn't want to get caught—what would I do next?"

I shook my head. "I don't know. Sorry. I haven't murdered enough people lately to know the answer to that question."

"I'd come up with an alibi," he said, ignoring my weak attempt at humor. "I'd go someplace very public as quickly as I could. Someplace I could claim I'd been during the murder. I certainly wouldn't go home, where no one could corroborate my whereabouts."

I frowned at him. "'Corroborate my whereabouts'? What were you before you moved to Eden? A lawyer?" I waved my hand at him. "I know, I know. Not allowed to ask." I stared into the bottom of my teacup, where the sediment had created an interesting pattern. Unfortunately, since I don't know how to read tea leaves, the closest I could make out was something that reminded me of a one-winged bird. And I had about as much chance of finding anything of importance in the bottom of a cup as that poor bird had to fly. None. Zero. Zilch.

"If you could stop feeling sorry for yourself for a few seconds, you'll see that I'm right," Gabe said gently. "Adam has no alibi because he doesn't need one, Hilde."

"Well, here's something you're not aware of, my know-it-all friend," I said. "Adam told me he had an appointment the morning of the murder and that it was canceled." I offered him my most superior look. "I talked to the secretary at his office. There was no appointment."

Gabe crossed his arms across his chest and leaned back in his chair. "You know, if you ever decide to use that mind of yours for good, we could all be in trouble." He shook his head and chuckled. "For your information, the appointment Adam had yesterday morning was at his dentist's office. The hygienist who was supposed to clean his teeth phoned in sick, and he had to reschedule." He grinned at me. "He mentioned it on the ride back to Eden."

I wanted to fire back something pithy, but my pithy supply was bone-dry. Adam had never said the appointment was work related; I'd just jumped to that conclusion. I glanced up at Gabe's wall clock. My commitment to trust Adam hadn't lasted long. But that woman. . .

Just then a soft alarm sounded. It was much quieter than the weather radio's raucous siren. Gabe got up and went into the living room to check his surveillance video screen. I heard him clomp down the stairs, and a couple of minutes later, he reappeared—with Adam.

Adam's face was flushed, his hair unruly, as if he'd been in a hurry to get here. He looked so good in his dark blue knit shirt and jeans that I had to gulp just to get my breathing back to normal. But even more appealing than his looks had always been his character. When I saw him walk into the kitchen, all I could think about was what an honest man he was—how much integrity I'd seen in him. Inside I felt ashamed for doubting him. But a niggling little demon of fear ran up and down my spine, warning me to be careful. Predicting pain ahead.

He leaned against the chair on the other side of the table. "You want to explain to me why you parked across the street from my house and then took off like a crazy person in front of my aunt Gertie?"

"That was your aunt?" was all I managed to squeak out.

He nodded slowly. "Aunt Gertie."

"Oh." I'd done it again. Flown off the handle and made a fool of myself. "Did you tell her who I was?"

"No. But she did mention that I might want to think about moving to a safer neighborhood where there aren't any 'hot-rodders' to contend with."

"Great. So if I ever meet your aunt, I'll have to buy a new car?"

"I doubt it, although your Cruiser probably added fuel to

the fire. It does kind of look like a hot rod."

Gabe wisely decided to stay out of the kitchen while Adam and I talked. My guess was that he could hear us anyway, but at least it seemed like we had a modicum of privacy. It gave me the strength to say what was on my heart.

"I'm sorry, Adam. I've tried so hard to trust you. It's a struggle for me. I think it's because. . ."

"Of your dad. I know." He pulled out the chair in front of him and sat down. "Hilde, I'm not your father. I have no idea why he left you and your mom, but I would never do that." His dark blue eyes sought mine. "I can't imagine the hurt a child feels when the person who is supposed to protect her turns his back and walks away. I don't want you to think I don't care—or I don't understand."

"You *don't* understand," I said, interrupting him. "Your parents have always been there for you. They've always supported you."

He nodded. "Yes. Yes, they have. And you're right. I don't know for certain how you feel, but if it's even half as devastating as I think it might be. . . Well, all I can say is, I'm sorry. I'm sorry for what you went through then, and I'm sorry for what you're going through now." He ran his hand through his long, dark hair and stared at the table. When he looked up at me, there were tears shining in his eyes. "Hilde, it's so unfair to ask you to trust me right now, with all this suspicion hanging over my head. I think we could work past your issues under normal circumstances. But with things the way they are now. . ."

"Adam, are you breaking up with me?"

He lowered his head and was silent for several seconds. Then he stood up and pushed his chair in. "I guess I am." His voice broke slightly and he cleared his throat. "I do love you, and I want to be with you. But this just doesn't seem to be the right time for us. Maybe after they find out who really killed Harold. . ." He offered me a small smile, but his eyes still held his pain. "When that happens, and it will, you'll have to do some soul-searching, Hilde. Either you live under the shadow of your father's actions, or you step out into a possible future with me. Right now there are three people in this relationship—and that can't possibly work." His eyes roamed over my face as if he was trying to memorize it. Then he turned and walked out. I wanted to run after him, but I was frozen in my chair. I heard him speak to Gabe briefly, and then I listened as his footsteps faded into the distance. The door downstairs closed, and a few moments after that, his car started and he drove away. This was the second time in one night I'd been confronted with my father's abandonment. Paula and Adam were right. My life was being ruined by the past.

"Is this what you really want?" Gabe stood in the doorway, his hands in his pockets, his expression somber.

I tried to blink back stubborn tears as I shook my head. "No. But he's right, Gabe. In all these years, I haven't gotten over what my father did. Maybe I don't have the ability to trust Adam. Maybe I can't trust anyone."

He smiled slowly. "But you say you trust God, Hilde."

"He's not a man. He can't lie and cheat."

Gabe grunted. "You're missing my point. If you really trusted Him, you'd put this relationship in His hands. Do you really believe He'd allow you to get involved with someone who would hurt you?"

"N–no."

"Then why don't you give the situation to Him? If this relationship isn't a blessing, you'll know before it's too late— if you'll listen with your heart."

I hung my head. "You're right. I've been trying to figure this out by myself. I obviously need help."

Gabe came over and sat down next to me. "And there's something else, Hilde." He took my hand in his. "You've got to forgive your father." I started to interrupt him, but he put his other hand up and tapped me lightly on the lips. "I know you think you've forgiven him. But if you really had, I don't believe you'd be dealing with all these bad feelings now."

I gently moved his hand away from my mouth. "I've said I've forgiven him so many times. I don't think I can say it anymore. I meant it when I said it the first time, but I can't control my emotions. The feelings come. All I can do is ask God to take them away."

"When do these feelings come? When you think about your dad?"

"Yes, I guess so."

He squeezed my hand. "But why are you thinking about the way he wronged you? I mean, if you've forgiven him. . ."

"You're asking me to control my thoughts?"

He smiled. "No, God asks you to control your thoughts. We're to take every thought captive and make it obedient to Christ. That means you don't have to take in everything that pops into your head. If you've really forgiven your father, the next time something about him starts to churn in your mind, shut it down and think about something else. Something good. Something praiseworthy."

"I don't see how that's going to change the way I feel."

"You'll find that our thoughts are the gateway to our emotions. You quit dwelling on the past, and God can move you into the future." He shook his head and stared at the floor. "Paul said, 'But one thing I do: Forgetting what is behind and straining toward what is ahead.'" His gaze locked on mine. "I don't know what I would have done if I hadn't had that scripture to hang on to. You know, Hilde, like Paul, a lot of people have things in their backgrounds that could ruin their lives if they thought about them all the time. Paul was party to a lot of persecution directed toward God's people. He overcame that by making a conscious decision to forget the past and concentrate on the future—with God. The only way that can happen is if we really understand forgiveness. God completely forgave us through Christ and gave us a fresh start—as if the past never existed. I know it sounds hard to do, but it isn't. Not really. Once you start to change your thinking and stop dwelling on things that have already happened, God gives you the grace to walk forward, free from the hurt and the anger. But you've got to take that first step." Gabe gave my hand a final squeeze and then got up to brew another pot of tea. I started to protest since I didn't want to be up all night, but before I could get a word out he smiled and said, "Caffeine free. You have nothing to worry about."

While he fussed around the stove, I thought about what he'd said. In my mind, I'd never really had a problem trusting God, but I hadn't truly given the situation with my father to Him. I hadn't trusted Him to take away the pain and heal me. Instead, I'd locked the hurt inside. I was learning the hard way that covering up emotional pain only causes more problems. And now I might have lost Adam because of it. I had to put the past where it belonged: in God's capable, loving hands.

"Adam's friends will be here tomorrow to start work on Ida Mae's house," Gabe said, abruptly pulling me out of my thoughts. "Hopefully, it won't rain all day."

That meant Adam would be back tomorrow. I had a lot of thinking ahead of me tonight, and it was already late. "Think I'll pass on that tea," I said. "I—I need some alone time."

Gabe moved the teapot off the burner. "I understand," he said. "Will you be around tomorrow?"

I stood up and stretched. My body felt tired, but my

mind was racing. "I have two jobs in the morning, but I should be back around noon."

"Good." He turned and walked into the living room. I followed him. "Why don't you swing by the Piccadilly Grill on your way into town? I'll order some box lunches for everyone."

Piccadilly is a great restaurant on the east side of Wichita. Not only does it have superb food; it houses a market that carries all kinds of hard-to-find foods and spices. "Do you know how many people will be here?" I asked.

He shrugged. "Adam said he had about fifteen men coming. Then there's you, me, Ida Mae, Butch, PeeWee, Derek, Mrs. Hudson, Minnie. . . Am I forgetting anyone?"

I grinned at him. "Yes, you forgot Watson."

He laughed. "Oh no, I haven't. I have a nice steak in the fridge with his name on it."

I shook my head. "That dog eats better than I do."

"Well, if you ever start licking my face and wagging your tail when you see me, I'll make you a steak, too." He thought for a moment and then winced. "On second thought, maybe not."

"Thank you. If I should ever do that, will you please just call someone and have me locked up?"

He leaned over and kissed the top of my head. "It will be my great pleasure."

I grunted. "I have no doubt about that."

I started to leave but stopped at the top of the stairs. "And Gabe?"

"Yes?"

"Thanks."

He smiled at me. "You're welcome. Just remember that nothing is too hard for God. He has everything you need. You just have to receive it."

I waved good-bye and headed home. I was glad I had my car, even if I only had to drive across the street. The rain was steady and cold. I parked in the long driveway, being careful not to block anyone else in. The carport was nothing more than a block of cement now, and we'd been told to stay away from it.

As I got out of the car, another vehicle rolled slowly down the street. Usually, the only people who drive through Eden live here. But I didn't recognize this car. It stopped between me and Gabe's house and sat there. I watched for a moment, but I had to run to the front porch to stay dry. When I turned around, the car, a dark-colored sedan, had pulled away. I had the strange feeling the driver had been watching me. I opened the door and went inside. The kitchen was empty, and I could hear the television coming from Mrs. Hudson's room. That meant she was probably already in bed. As I crept quietly up the stairs, I tried to put the strange car out of my mind. I needed some time with my Father—the One who promised He'd never leave me nor forsake me. We had a lot to talk about. I spent the next few hours curled up on my window seat, wrapped in my grandmother's homemade quilt, watching the rain and talking to my very best friend. Eventually, I fell asleep, wrapped in the arms of love.

CHAPTER ▐▌▐▐▌ TEN

Wednesday morning dawned with clear skies, but the weather report that squawked from my grandmother's ancient radio promised another round of storms later that night. Not unusual for this time of year, but I was getting a little tired of being soaked. I love rain and snow, but it appeals to me more when I watch it from my window seat. Running around in it can be a little problematic. Especially when you live out in the country.

I got ready for work, said good-bye to Sherlock, and hurried downstairs. Mrs. Hudson, Minnie, and Ida Mae were all in the kitchen. Mrs. Hudson and Ida Mae were deeply involved in a discussion about books. But Minnie sat silently in her chair, her brightly colored hair framing an expression that was about as friendly as a pit bull in a tutu. It appeared Miss Minnie desperately needed instructions on how to play well with others.

I stopped at the entrance to the kitchen and waited for a break in their conversation. Finally, Mrs. Hudson took notice of me.

"Why, Hilde! I didn't see you there. How about some

breakfast? I made a nice coffee cake."

"No, thank you," I said with a smile. "I just wanted to tell you that I'll be bringing lunch back from town. Gabe asked me to pick up sandwiches from Piccadilly."

Mrs. Hudson put her hand to her cheek. "I'm so glad you told me. I was trying to think of what I could put together to feed everyone."

"Well, we won't need anything today. I imagine having something to drink would be helpful, though."

She clapped her hands together. "That's no problem at all. I'll make some lemonade and have the coffeemaker going when you get back."

"The least I can do is to help you, Arabella," Ida Mae said. "Goodness, you all are going to so much trouble to help me. I—I just can't believe it."

Mrs. Hudson shook her head. "That's what neighbors are for. Isn't it too bad people today don't expect their neighbors to share their burdens? Why, back in my day—"

"I'll see you all later," I interjected. I hated to interrupt, but when Mrs. Hudson started one of her "back in my day" stories, you might as well settle in for a while—and I just didn't have the time.

Ida Mae and Mrs. Hudson each chimed out a high-pitched "Good-bye, Hilde!" while Minnie just looked daggers at me. As I walked past the doorway, I shot her a warning glance. Seeing her eyes widen told me that she knew exactly what I meant. Minnie and I have had several conversations about her attitude, and I had no intention of allowing her to do or say anything that might hurt Ida Mae. To her benefit, Minnie had admitted on more than one occasion that she sometimes allowed herself to slip into unhealthy thought patterns. "My mother was a complainer, Hilde," she'd explained to me. "Nothing was ever right for that woman. Sometimes I find myself acting just like her. And I don't like it at all." She'd grasped my arm with her stoplight red, chipped nails. "If you ever see me doing that, will you let me know? She was such an unhappy woman. I don't want to end up the same way." Unfortunately, reminding her of her desire to stay positive was almost a full-time job. I kept hoping Mrs. Hudson would rub off on her. Mrs. Hudson was happiest when she was helping others, whereas Minnie was happiest when she was being helped.

I pushed the front door open and stepped out into the kind of day that makes me want to breathe the joy of springtime deep inside myself. Although snowy winters are my favorite time of year, this kind of day could almost make me rethink my preferences. It was perfect for working outside, and I thanked God for sending it.

It took me a little longer than I'd planned to get through my second appointment. My client's hair had thinned dramatically because of a long period of poor health. To give her back her pre-illness look, I used a wig sent by her family. Unfortunately, it looked unnatural, and I had to rework it to make it look like real hair. By the time I finished, the funeral home staff was very happy with the results, but I was running about fifteen minutes behind. I hurried over to Piccadilly to find that everything was ready to go. A helpful employee loaded up the boxes and took them to my car. I was on my way without any hassles whatsoever. Piccadilly's exceptional service got me back on track, and I got to Eden right at twelve thirty.

Mrs. Hudson stood waiting next to some card tables set up under a large oak tree. A couple of the men ran over to help me unload all the boxes and carry them to the tables. After sorting them by sandwich type, Mrs. Hudson asked me to watch over things while she and Ida Mae got the coffee and made another gallon of lemonade. There were already several foam cups with ice and lemonade waiting for thirsty workers.

I was happy to serve the food until she could get back. If he got hungry enough, Adam would have no choice but to face me. I looked around for him, but I didn't see him at first. Finally, he strolled from around the back of Ida Mae's house. I wanted desperately to talk to him, but I was afraid to approach him on my own. I wasn't sure if he wanted anything to do with me.

I'd just handed a box with a turkey sandwich to PeeWee when someone put his hand on my shoulder. I turned around to find Ernie "BooBoo" Carson smiling at me.

"How are you, Hilde?" he asked. His rather guarded smile told me he knew things weren't quite right between

Adam and me. Ernie, a small, wiry man who works as a prison guard, had known Adam for a long time. In fact, it was Ernie who first introduced Clowns for Christ to his high school friend.

"I–I'm fine, Ernie. How about you and the boys?"

Ernie's wife, Maggie, had passed away almost a year ago. I knew it had been a tough year for Ernie and his two children. "We're doing okay. Most days it just comes down to putting one foot in front of the other."

Just then Butch stepped up next to us. "Ham, turkey, or chicken salad?" I asked him.

"Chicken salad sounds just right. Sure was nice of that Mr. Bashevis, buying all this food."

"Yes, it was. But it isn't anywhere near enough for everything you're doing."

He colored and shook his head as I handed him a box marked CKN SALAD and a plastic cup full of homemade lemonade. "Shucks, this is just what neighbors do, Hilde. Anyway, it's what they did back in my day."

As he thanked me and walked away, I wondered how old he was. His sentiments mirrored Mrs. Hudson's, almost word for word. Seemed to me they were about the same age. Butch had been alone almost as long as she had. An urge to do a little matchmaking stared to swirl around in my brain.

"Sure has been a terrible week for our group," Ernie said, pulling me out of my plans to wean Mrs. Hudson from Gabe and focus her in a new direction. He reached past me and took one of the ham sandwiches. Then he sat down on a folding chair that leaned up against the tree. "First we lose Marvin—now Harold. It's a lot to process."

I pulled up another chair. "Ernie, I've noticed some of the guys staring at Adam. Do they think—I mean, have they heard. . ."

"Have they heard that Adam's been accused of killing Harold?" He shrugged and looked at me. "That kind of news spreads pretty fast." He wolfed down a bite of his sandwich then wiped his mouth with his sleeve. "No one who really knows him believes it, Hilde, if that's what you're asking. There's no way he could have killed Harold—or anyone. Besides, why would he? It doesn't make any sense." He stared down at his dirty work boots and began trying to scrape off some of the mud on the grass. "None of us can come up with a reason to kill Harold. My goodness, that man would have taken the shirt off his back for anyone who asked. Back when he was running his furniture store, he was always helping people out. I remember when Maggie and I got married. 'You come in and pick out any furniture you want, Ernie,'" he said. "'You pay me back as you can. If it takes awhile, that's okay by me.'" Ernie smiled slowly. "It took us almost a year and a half to settle our account—and I know he only charged us half of what the stuff was worth. He always acted surprised when we brought in a payment. 'Are you sure about this?' he'd ask. 'I'm not in any hurry.'"

"Adam still has a couch he bought from Harold when he

graduated from college. He almost had to force him to take his money."

"That sounds just like Harold," Ernie said sadly. "It's so hard to believe he's gone. And then there's Marvin. Goodness, I have so much to thank him for. You know, he pressured Maggie and me to buy life insurance for about a year before we gave in and did it. At first we thought he was just trying to make money off us. He'd been retired for about five years by then, but he kept his license so he could take care of his friends. Once we figured out that he was trying to help us, we took out two policies. It was kind of expensive, but Marvin convinced us that we owed it to our kids to make sure there would be money if anything ever happened to us." He sighed and stared over my shoulder as if observing something I couldn't see. "Maggie died in that car wreck about six months after we signed for that insurance. I can't imagine what I would have done without the money. Me and the boys have no financial worries because Marvin worked so hard to make sure we were safe." He picked up his sandwich and took another bite that disappeared almost as fast as it went into his mouth. "I loved both those guys. I know Marvin's death was an accident, but Harold's wasn't. I sure would like to find the dirtbag that killed him. But one thing I know. It wasn't Adam."

"It certainly *wasn't* Adam," a deep voice said from behind me. Billy "Buttons" Larkin walked up to the table. I was surprised to see him. Billy worked as an insurance investigator. He spent a lot of time out of town and performed the least with the group. Although some of the men were retired, there were several who were still employed. To keep the members from burning themselves out, there were several smaller groups inside the larger troupe. All in all, there were four bands of clowns that took turns at the various hospitals and events. That made it easier for Billy to get the chance to don his clown suit and entertain children with the rest of his friends. Although I didn't know Billy as well as the other guys, I liked him. He was friendly and seemed to be consistently happy—in spite of the fact that his wife appeared to be rather high-maintenance. Adam told me that none of the men liked her, that she was always taking advantage of Billy, who did everything he could to please her. Mindy had grown up in a wealthy family and expected Billy to provide the lavish lifestyle she was accustomed to. So besides his regular job, he also sold funeral services for Slumberland. Although the other men in Clowns for Christ knew about his sideline, according to Adam, he'd never approached any of them about the plans, preferring not to mix ministry with business. One of the group's members did buy a plan from Billy, but he almost had to force Billy to sell it to him. And Ernie had used Slumberland's lower-cost services when Maggie died. But Marvin's family had gone with Willowbrook, the most prestigious home in Wichita.

"Amen, brother," Ernie intoned right before he shoved the rest of his sandwich in his mouth. For a small man, he was quite an energetic eater. He tossed his empty box into the trash can Mrs. Hudson had placed a few feet away from the food table. Ernie stared at me, his eyebrows knit together and his arms folded across his chest. "I know a few of the guys wonder about the charges against Adam, but his real friends will stand by him, Hilde. I hope you do, too. I've never seen him as happy as he's been since you came into his life." He shook his head. "Building a relationship takes a lot of work—and trust." His gravelly voice softened. "But when you've found the right person, it's worth every second of it. No matter how much effort you put into it, you get blessed back in spades." He stared down at the ground for a minute. When he looked up, his eyes were shiny. "Don't give up on him, okay?"

I smiled at him. "I won't. Pray he doesn't give up on me, either."

"I'll do that." He glanced up at the sky. "Looks like we better get busy. More rain expected later." He got up and walked off.

Billy took the seat Ernie left vacant. His hawkish good looks were crowned with a haircut that used to be called a flattop. Although I was drawn to men with longer hair, it wasn't hard to see why his younger, attractive wife found him physically appealing.

He pulled out his sandwich and took a bite, chewing a little longer than Ernie had. It wasn't only the way he ate that made him different than the chair's previous occupant.

Ernie's clothes were made for hard work and spotted with paint stains. Billy's jeans were designed to look casual. His long-sleeved chambray shirt was obviously expensive. I doubted if Mindy allowed him to wear the kind of torn-up, well-used clothes that Ernie and most of the other guys were so comfortable with. I found myself feeling a little sorry for him.

"How about some lemonade?" I asked him.

"Sounds great," he said. "The weather's nice and cool, but working up a sweat can still make you thirsty."

I took a cup over to him and sat down. Adam was still working and hadn't made a move to get lunch. I hoped he was just busy and not avoiding me. Billy caught me looking at Adam.

"So you and Adam are having problems?"

I couldn't lie, but I didn't really want to get into our personal problems. "There's been a lot of stress lately with Marvin's and Harold's deaths."

He sighed deeply. "I'll say. You know, since this group got started, we've lost a couple of other guys. Both natural causes. A lot of our members are pretty old. But Marvin was only sixty, and Harold was sixty-two. They both retired early so they could spend time with their families and put more effort into the group. Sure doesn't seem fair."

"No. It's not fair. You're right about that."

He took another bite of his sandwich then chewed and swallowed it. "Guess the good Lord decided it was time to take them home."

I didn't respond. "The good Lord" certainly wasn't into electrocuting and murdering His children.

"I heard the police questioned Adam," he continued. "I couldn't believe it. Why in the world would they think he had anything to do with Harold's death?"

"Some guy who works at the cemetery saw a red car that looked like Adam's parked near the place where Harold's body was found."

Billy's jaw dropped. "And that's it? That's absolutely ridiculous." He shook his head in disbelief. "I can't believe it. Two of my friends gone and another one suspected of killing them. It's absurd."

"I think I heard that you and Marvin had known each other a long time."

He put his sandwich down and his expression turned serious. "That's true. In fact, he helped me get my first job. He wanted me to sell insurance, like he did. But I'm just not the salesman type." He looked at me and smiled. "I know. I sell funeral services, but that's a little different. I just let people know I work with Slumberland. I don't try to get them to buy from me. People come to me on their own because they really want to make sure they're prepared for what they know will come someday. Doesn't take the kind of sales pitch life insurance and annuities take." He shrugged. "Anyway, that's how I look at it. But when Marvin told me about being an insurance investigator, it piqued my interest.

I've been doing it ever since."

"I didn't know Marvin very well," I said. "I only met him a few times, but he was always nice to me. Always made me feel welcome and a part of the group."

"That was Marvin." He shook his head. "I wish I'd been with him that day. Maybe he would still be alive."

"I never did understand why the electricity was still on in that house," I said. "Didn't he know enough to make sure it was off?"

A look of pain flashed across his face, and he hesitated. "Look, Hilde," he said, lowering his voice. "I don't want you to repeat this, but Marvin had been getting a little forgetful lately. I'm not the only person who noticed it. Harold was concerned about it, too." Billy looked around, probably checking to see if anyone else could hear him. "I don't want to make his family think it was anything more than a simple mistake. I'm afraid if they know he was having real problems, they'll wonder if they should have done something about it. You know, like protect him or something." He shook his head again. "No reason for anyone to start blaming themselves for an accident."

"Sure doesn't seem that complicated, though," I said. "Turning off the breaker switches should be a matter of routine."

"It should be," he said, nodding. "And I understand that some of them were turned off. Just not the right one." He sighed. "That breaker box shouldn't have been placed under the stairs where there was no direct lighting. Even if Marvin didn't forget to flip the switches, he could have easily missed the right one because he couldn't see it well enough." He shrugged. "I guess we'll never know what really happened. At least he went out the way he lived. Helping people."

"Are all the guys in the group wearing their costumes to Marvin's funeral?"

He nodded. "You bet. Out of respect for Marvin. To the funeral and to the cemetery for the graveside service."

I shuddered. "It will feel a little strange to go back to Shady Rest after finding Harold's body there."

"Sorry. I guess Maria can't move it because the rest of their family is buried there. I've never been to Shady Rest. Most people pick Eternal Gardens. I think it's a lot newer."

I nodded. "Shady Rest has been around a long, long time." I started to say something else, but I noticed Adam looking our way. After staring for several seconds, he put his shovel down and began walking toward the food table.

"Guess I'd better get back to work," Billy said. Apparently he'd also noticed Adam advancing on us. He took a couple of big bites of his sandwich, put the rest back in the box, and tossed the box in the trash. Then he stood up. "I'll just take this lemonade to go."

I smiled at him. "Thanks, Billy. I appreciate it."

He winked at me. "No problem. We all want to see you and Adam together. He needs you."

He headed back to work, passing Adam, who appeared

to be walking about as slow as a human being can without stopping altogether.

When he finally reached the table, he just stood there, awkwardly shifting from one foot to the other. In his paint-stained jeans and powder blue T-shirt, he reminded me of a shy teenager getting ready to ask for a first date. Not a successful stockbroker, used to handling large amounts of money for well-to-do clients.

"Hi, Hilde," he said finally. "This is a nice thing for you to do. Serving lunch, I mean."

"Gabe bought it," I said inanely. "And Ida Mae and Mrs. Hudson made the lemonade." Great conversation. Maybe we could start in on the weather next.

"Pretty clear right now," he said, squinting at the sky. "But I heard we're in for some more rain."

"Oh, for crying out loud!"

Adam's eyebrows shot up. "What's the matter with you now?"

I slapped the table with the flat of my hand. "I don't want to discuss the weather with you," I said. "We have more serious things to talk about."

Out of the corner of my eye, I could see several of the men looking our way.

Adam's face turned red. "What is there to say, Hilde?"

I stepped around the table and stood inches away from him. "How about this? You were right. You were right about everything. I *have* been living under the shadow of my father.

I've been judging you based on his actions, and I've been wrong. Wrong, wrong, wrong. But I'm ready to move on, Adam. I love you, and I'm ready to trust you completely." I had to take a deep breath to continue. "If you'll let me, I'd like to help you figure out who really killed. . ."

I didn't get the chance to finish my sentence before Adam grabbed me and kissed me so hard I was glad I'd taken that breath first.

CHAPTER ELEVEN

By the time it got too dark to see, we'd cleared away almost all the remaining debris. There were still a couple of piles that Butch said he'd haul away in the morning. Although the promised storm hadn't yet arrived, I could feel moisture in the air. In the distance, the sky had begun to flash with lightning, although it looked to be a few hours away from us. I was grateful it had held off long enough for us to finish our work.

Adam, Gabe, and I gathered over at Gabe's place for dinner—and to recoup. Thankfully, Gabe still had some leftovers in his fridge from a casserole I'd cooked several days ago. Potatoes, green peppers, onions, cheese, and SPAM with Bacon. It was good the first time and even better warmed up. Gabe heated up some croissants to go along with it. We were exhausted but happily full by the time the last spoonful was scooped out of the pan.

"I'm almost too tired to drive home," Adam said. His excessive blinking and bleary eyes agreed.

"You can stay here tonight," Gabe said. "The love seat

in the living room makes out to a bed." He glanced toward the living room where Watson had found a comfortable spot in the corner and was snoring happily. "Watson's already claimed his spot."

"Well, if you let me use your toothbrush, you might have a deal," Adam said with a grin.

Gabe grunted. "How about a new toothbrush? I have several under the sink. You can help yourself." He looked up and down at Adam's dirty clothes. "I have some extra pajamas, too. We'll throw your clothes in the washer so they'll be clean in the morning."

"What about work?" I asked. "I assume you took today off, but what about tomorrow morning?"

"I took the whole week off," Adam said. "With helping Ida Mae and the funeral tomorrow, I figured I'd need all the time I could get." He yawned. "Gabe, if your offer is serious, I might really crash here tonight. If Hilde can take me by my place in the morning to change, we shouldn't have any trouble making it to the service on time." He stared at me with bloodshot eyes. "It starts at ten, right?"

I nodded. "Yep. Ten o'clock." I stretched my legs and groaned. "Right now, that sounds way too early to get up, get dressed, and try to look presentable. I'd rather spend the day recovering."

"There's a reception at the Martinezes' church after the service," Adam said, stifling another yawn. "Some of us will attend, and the rest of the group will spend the afternoon working on Ida Mae's house. If we get back soon enough, we can help. Boy, my muscles don't feel ready to go at it again, but we need to get that roof on as soon as possible. Those tarps are no match for a strong storm."

I groaned and shook my head. "I think you guys need a supervisor. Maybe I'll watch from the sidelines and criticize you at appropriate times."

It was Gabe's turn to chuckle. "Very helpful. Your dedication is impressive."

"Thank you very much," I said with a wave of my hand. "I am nothing if not committed."

"I think you mean you should *be* committed," Adam said.

"Yeah, that, too." With effort, I straightened up in my chair. "Before we wrapped up for the night, I noticed you seemed to be in a pretty deep conversation with Ernie. What was all that about?"

Before Adam had a chance to answer, Gabe's teakettle began to whistle. We waited while he took it off the stove. "Chamomile tea," he said with a smile. "The perfect way to end the day." He poured the hot water into his teapot. Then he put the tea mixture into a mesh infuser shaped like a ball and placed it inside the pot. He picked up the kettle and poured the hot water over the infuser. "Let this steep for a few minutes. You'll love it, and it will help relax you."

A delicious aroma wafted through the room. Patience not being one of my virtues, I didn't intend to let it sit long.

Hopefully, Adam's conversation with Ernie would provide some distraction.

"So what about Ernie?" I said.

"Well, it was very interesting," Adam said with a shake of his head. "And it wasn't only Ernie. Several of the guys took me aside to tell me their theories as to who killed Harold."

"Spill it," I said sharply. "What did you find out?"

Gabe laughed. "Mellow out, Miss Marple. Give the poor guy a chance."

"That's okay," Adam said with a grin. "I'm getting used to being shoved around by a woman. I think I'm starting to like it."

I sighed as loudly as I could. "You're both quite entertaining. Now what did they say to you? We're trying to keep you out of the pokey, you know."

Adam's face lost its previous jovial expression. "Point taken," he said. "You asked about Ernie. Nice guy. We've been friends a long time. I know he had a hard time telling me this, but he felt he had to because of my. . .situation."

Gabe sat down at the table. "What did he say, Adam?"

Adam hesitated. I reached over and put my hand on his arm. "I know you don't like to gossip, but this isn't the time to keep anything back. We need to know the truth."

Adam put his hand over mine. "It seems that Harold's wife talked him into increasing his life insurance policy a short time before he was killed. She stands to inherit a great deal of money. Ernie wasn't sure how much it is, but he heard that it was over a million dollars."

The news left me stunned. "Harold's wife? Betty? You think she killed him for the insurance money?" I'd met her several times at various functions. She seemed very nice and completely devoted to Harold. It was hard to think of her as a cold-blooded murderer.

"I'm not finished," he said. "Albert Collins told me that he overheard Betty and Harold in a real knock-down, drag-out argument at the potluck dinner last month. He doesn't know what the fight was about, but he heard Betty tell Harold that he needed to 'tell the truth' about something he got in the mail."

"Maybe Harold was fooling around," Gabe said helpfully. "Another woman sent him a love letter."

"Oh, come on," I sputtered. "Betty is a murderer and Harold is an adulterer? I don't believe that for one minute. They're great, Christian people. There's no way. . ."

Adam looked at me like he'd never seen me before. "Oh, but I'm capable of killing one of my best friends with a shovel and dumping his body into the grave of another close friend?"

I folded my arms across my chest and scowled at him. "You're going to have to get over that little mistake if we have any hope of a future."

His eyes widened and his mouth dropped open. Then he started to laugh. Gabe joined in.

"Never try to figure out women, Adam," he said, shaking

his head. "No matter what you do, you can't win."

I waited patiently until they calmed down. "If you're both ready to get on with it?"

Adam patted my hand. "Okay. Sorry. But sometimes you're really cute."

"You won't have much to laugh about in jail."

"All right, all right." He stared down at the table. "Where was I. . ."

"Albert Collins. And Harold with a floozy on the side."

"A *floozy*?" Gabe said.

I shrugged. "Heard the term in an old movie."

"For crying out loud. What kind of movies do you watch?" Adam asked.

"Get on with it," I said pointedly. "This is serious."

"You're right. This is serious," Adam said, fighting a grin. Gabe covered his mouth with his hand.

"You two are useless." I stood up. "You're both so tired, you're goofy. Maybe we'd better talk about this tomorrow. I'm exhausted, too, you know."

"I'm sorry," Adam said. "Sit down. I won't fool around anymore."

I looked at Gabe, who nodded his agreement.

"You said several people talked to you. What else did you hear?"

"Well, Mark Schneider, he was Harold's dentist, told me that Harold had an appointment to get a filling about a week before he died. Mark said Harold was jumpy and short-tempered the whole time he was in his chair. Mark had never seen him like that. Harold was clearly upset about something."

"I'd be upset, too, if I was having my teeth drilled," I said.

"But Harold was the kind of man who always took things in stride. His actions that day were out of character."

"Adam," Gabe said, "when did you have your run-in with him?"

"That's exactly what I was going to point out," Adam said. "Harold's appointment with Mark was in the morning. He saw me the afternoon of the same day. He couldn't have been angry with both of us. He must have been troubled—worried. If we can figure out what was bothering him, maybe we can solve his murder."

I sighed. "But the only leads we have so far are that Betty increased Harold's life insurance and wanted her husband to tell the truth about something? That's not very convincing evidence of murder. A lot of people Harold's and Betty's age increase their life insurance. And I'll bet most wives would like their husbands to be more truthful."

Gabe got up and removed the tea filter from the pot. Then he carried the pot over to the table. "How many in your group are insurance agents?" he asked Adam. "Sounds like you're overrun with them."

Adam pushed his cup toward Gabe, who filled it. Then he poured a cup for me and one for himself. He put the pot on the table and sat down again.

"There are several men who work in insurance," Adam said. "Remember that most of our members come in through people they already know. Many of them have worked together in some capacity." He took a sip of his tea. "We have about five or six guys in insurance, a few in real estate, some contractors, and quite a few who own businesses."

I tasted my tea, blowing on it first to cool it. "This is delicious, Gabe," I said. "You're right. It is the perfect way to end a long, hard day."

"I thought you'd like it," Gabe said, smiling.

"Is that it, Adam?" My eyelids were beginning to feel like they weighed more than the rest of me.

"No. There's something else. Something rather odd."

"What's that?" I asked, pushing back a yawn.

"Even though Harold retired from his furniture business and left his son in charge, he kept an office in the building. He liked to go down there from time to time to see how things were going. He still had a controlling interest in the store."

"So?"

"So BoBo. . .I mean, Terry Nicholson, told me he was in the store last Thursday morning looking at new bedroom furniture for his daughter. He saw Marvin there."

"So? What's odd about that?" I didn't want to sound rude, but I was too tired to follow rabbit trails that went nowhere.

"Don't snap at me."

"Sorry, but could you get to the point before I pass out?"

"The point is that Terry heard Marvin and Harold shouting at each other. He said it was a pretty heated argument. Unfortunately, he couldn't hear what they were fighting about."

"Wait a minute," Gabe said. "When did Marvin die?"

"Thursday afternoon," Adam said.

"So Marvin and Harold get into an argument on Thursday morning, Marvin dies that afternoon, and Harold is killed a few days later?" My brain had snapped to attention. Any feelings of weariness disappeared.

"I hadn't really thought about it until now," Adam said with a frown. "But that's a real coincidence, isn't it?"

"I would say so," Gabe said. The seriousness of his tone matched the look on his face as he stared at Adam. "Maybe your friend Marvin's death wasn't an accident at all. He may have been murdered."

CHAPTER TWELVE

Sitting through a clown funeral is an experience I wouldn't wish on my worst enemy. Or my best friend. Paula only lasted ten minutes before she left the chapel with her hand over her mouth in an attempt to stifle her giggles. I shot her a dirty look on her way out, but that only seemed to make it worse.

I sat through the entire service not knowing whether to laugh or cry. The tributes from the other clowns were quite touching, and the stories about some of the children whose lives had been impacted through Clowns for Christ brought tears to my eyes more than once. I certainly wasn't the only one. These great vignettes were marred only by the fact that they were being delivered by grown men in ludicrous costumes and garish makeup. I found it hard to listen to BoBo, B.B., BooBoo, Bingo, and Bucky talk about the seriousness of Marvin's commitment. It was even tougher to hear from Buttercup, my Adam, in a red wig and clown makeup, dressed in a red jacket and yellow shirt, with a big plastic flower attached to his lapel.

I only caught glimpses of Maria Martinez from my seat in the back of the chapel, but she appeared to take the odd components of the service in stride. A few rows behind her, I noticed Betty Tuttwiler sitting with her son. She was an attractive woman who carried herself with dignity and class, and I wondered if she was thinking about Harold's upcoming funeral. I had my doubts that his service would be clown infused.

My emotions swung from sadness to an almost overwhelming desire to laugh. With no small effort, I made it through the service without embarrassing myself.

Afterward, as Adam and I were walking to my car so we could get in line for the procession to the cemetery, we were hailed by Billy, dressed in his "Buttons" costume.

"Can we ride over with you?" he asked, holding on to Mindy's hand and dragging her along. "After all that rain last night, I don't want to take my car out in the mud."

Billy's expensive foreign car was his pride and joy. In my opinion, the midsize green automobile wasn't anything to write home about. It didn't look much different than a lot of American cars, but Billy treated it like it was a treasured child.

"Sure, but how will you get back here after the reception?" Adam asked.

Billy waved his gloved hand dismissively. "Several of the guys live on this side of town. We won't have any trouble getting a ride."

Mindy didn't seem too happy. Either she was put out that she wouldn't be riding in luxury to the cemetery or she was simply appalled by the entire situation. She didn't appear to be as clown-friendly as her devoted husband. With a rather sour expression, she followed us to my car. After casting a suspicious look toward my Cruiser, Mindy climbed in, and we all headed for Shady Rest with Adam driving. It felt somewhat surreal to return to the "scene of the crime," so to speak, and bury Marvin in the grave where Harold's body had been discovered. I said as much to the other occupants of the car.

"Actually, Betty asked for a different burial site in the same area," Billy said. "The family owns several plots in that section. She was able to keep Harold near the rest of the family, but she didn't have to use that particular plot. My understanding is that it will remain unused out of respect for Harold."

I thought back to my previous visit to Shady Rest. My photographic memory kicked in, and I could see the same family name on several of the headstones. "Didn't seem to be any unused spots near Marvin's original site," I said. "Wonder where he'll be now."

"I believe it's on the other side of the stone bench," Billy said thoughtfully. "Maria said something about wanting to be able to sit near his grave."

The idea of Maria sitting alone on that bench, mourning Marvin, made me sad. My mother and I visit my grandmother's grave every year and put silk flowers in the metal vase attached to her marker. I don't feel her there, though. It's only when I snuggle up in the quilt she made for me that it seems as if she's close. Maybe it would be different for Maria. Everyone grieves in her own way, I guess.

Shady Rest is about five miles from the funeral home. Not too far if you're driving normally, but in a funeral procession, it seems to take forever. To break the silence, I tried to engage Mindy in conversation. Unfortunately, I had very little success. After asking her a few questions about how she spent her time, I finally gave up. Her sparkling dialogue consisted of "I dunno," "Nothin'," and her one rather long diatribe about how she likes to spend Saturdays at the mall and what her favorite stores are. Of course, she didn't ask one single question about me or Adam. Carrying on one-sided conversations is not only hard; it's almost impossible.

Adam, who could tell I was sinking fast, asked Billy about his job. I was thankful that Billy was able to come up with some interesting stories dealing with insurance fraud. I had no idea so many people tried to get funds from insurance companies with false claims.

"How did you get started as an investigator, Billy?" I asked.

"I spent a few years as a cop," he said. "But I wasn't interested in writing traffic tickets. Too boring. Marvin knew I wanted a change, so he told me about a job opening in investigations. When I said I was interested, he recommended me, and I got hired by an insurance company—in their SIU. That means Special Investigations Unit. I get sent out whenever a large property loss seems suspicious."

"What kind of loss?"

"A lot of fire cases. In fact, I'm kind of a fire specialist."

Mindy sighed loudly. It was clear she'd heard all this before and couldn't have been more bored. But Billy's line of work was fascinating to me.

"What do you look for when you investigate a fire?" I asked.

"Pour patterns," Billy said. "When an accelerant is used to start a fire, it forms a pattern. Also, fire burns up and out. It causes a V-shaped pattern. Most arsonists don't know that. If the patterns don't look right at the scene of a fire, we have possible evidence of arson."

"Billy's brought quite a few people to justice," Adam said. "Right, Billy?"

"Well, actually, getting anyone convicted of a criminal action is tough," he said. "Unless someone actually sees them set the fire, a lot of courts won't prosecute. Usually, my company will file a civil case. If we win that, the insured doesn't get paid—and they have to pick up our court costs. Sometimes, if the claim has already been paid, they have to give the money back. In fact, I'm looking at a case right now where a guy might have set his business on fire. He got paid for his claim, but I've found some evidence that might cause that claim to be overturned. He may have to return a little over a million dollars to his insurance company."

I was so interested in Billy's story that I didn't even notice we'd reached the cemetery. Our procession slowed down and then stopped so we could turn into Shady Rest. The funeral guards on motorcycles blocked traffic coming from the other direction.

"This place is kind of a dump," Billy said as we passed through the first section of gravesites. "Of course, Maria said their family bought their plots over seventy years ago. This was probably the best cemetery in town back then."

"We bought plots at Eternal Gardens," Mindy said, her nasal voice emphasizing her attempt to denigrate Shady Rest.

Eternal Gardens Cemetery is only about ten years old. Its carefully sculpted grounds and large, lighted statues have helped it to become the *pièce de résistance* among the dead and buried crowd. Frankly, I prefer Shady Rest. The stone and bronze headstones have more character than the flat, bronze grave markers everyone is compelled to use at Eternal Gardens. It's hard to believe that even cemeteries have housing codes.

We followed the lead limousine and the hearse to the spot where a tent stood waiting for the brief burial ceremony. Most of us had to park a long way from the location. The ground was still muddy from the torrential rains over the last few days.

"It's worse than I imagined," Billy grumbled as we carefully traipsed our way toward Marvin's site.

Mindy's constant sighs of exasperation helped to create

an odd cacophony with the sucking sounds we made by pulling our feet out of the mud as we walked. I wanted to mention that wearing seven-hundred-dollar Italian leather shoes to a muddy cemetery wasn't the brightest thing to do, but I just smiled and clumped through the muck and mire in my twenty-dollar discount-shoe-store specials. I tried to keep from searching for the original plot picked for Marvin, but I had to look. The grave had been filled up. The new plot was in the same area yet far enough away from the scene of Harold's murder to keep it from being creepy.

We finally reached our destination. Although quite a few chairs had been set up next to the gravesite, many people still had to stand. Being among the last to arrive, we missed out on seats. I made it a point to look at Marvin's headstone. Sure enough, a clown hat rested there. I wondered if it was the original hat. Since that had probably been kept as evidence, my guess was that this was a substitute.

Adam clomped over to where the coffin sat on top of the lowering device, his big rubber shoes caked with mud. The other men, all dressed in costume, stood in a semicircle around their departed comrade. My previous bout with the giggles completely disappeared. It was clear these men loved each other and cared deeply about sick and disadvantaged children. They were willing to dress up and look silly just to give these kids something to smile about. I realized they epitomized the scripture about becoming "fools for Christ," and in that moment, my lifelong revulsion for clowns disintegrated. I felt proud of Adam—proud of all of them. I mourned Marvin, a funny little man who spent his life helping others. And Harold, a big man with an even bigger heart. He was the very first member of Adam's group I ever met. From the very beginning, he'd gone out of his way to make me feel welcome. He'd always call out, "Hi there, Hildee-dee-dee!" when I walked into a room. I'd always found it annoying. Suddenly, though, it seemed sweet and endearing, and I wished with all my heart I could hear him say it again.

Adam kept glancing at me while each man recounted a memory from his relationship with Marvin. I'm sure he was wondering why I'd become so emotional. Even though the stories were touching, and many people wiped away tears, he knew I'd hardly spent any time at all with Marvin. All I could do was smile at Adam and blot my face with my sleeve. Mindy, on the other hand, appeared to be hiding her face from an invisible camera. She was obviously embarrassed by the proceedings, yet she'd known Marvin and his wife much longer than I had.

Finally, the men finished and stepped away from the coffin. They formed a line at one end, reminiscent of soldiers at a military funeral, each standing at attention, ramrod straight, staring ahead.

Mindy leaned over and whispered rather loudly, "Man, I thought clowns were supposed to be funny!"

Several people turned toward us. Now it was my turn to

look embarrassed. From the front row, someone stood up. It was Maria Martinez, Marvin's wife. A small, stocky woman, she had a reputation for keeping her family in line. Yet today, she looked like any other grieving widow. She walked over to her husband's coffin and turned toward the gathered crowd. From the expression on the pastor's face, her impromptu speech wasn't part of the program. I had to wonder if she was reacting to Mindy's comment.

"I know the way we've conducted my husband's funeral seems strange to many of you," she said, attempting to speak loudly enough for everyone to hear. "In fact, some of the members of my family were against holding a service like this. At first, I felt the same way—that it wasn't respectful or dignified. But then I realized that my husband deserved the kind of funeral he wanted. I've come to realize that dressing up like a clown and making children laugh was more than just something he was interested in. It was his ministry. Some of you may have important jobs and impressive titles. But Marvin was a man who cared more about giving than taking and more about serving than being served." Her voice broke. She hesitated a moment and then began again, her voice controlled and strong. "For those of you who don't understand why I decided to honor my husband's request, I'm sorry. I want to make it clear that I am not apologizing for my choice—or for Marvin's. I am sorry for you, that you have so little understanding of what's really important. You see"—she waved her hand toward the assembled clowns— "these men are proud of what they do. And they should be.

And I'm proud to be a part of them." At this, she reached into her jacket pocket and took out a large, red rubber ball, which she stuck on her nose. Perhaps there should have been some laughter, but there was only silence. As she went back to her seat, one by one, the men standing to the side of Marvin's casket began to clap. Then the rest of us joined in. In my almost two years of working with funeral homes and attending various services, I found this strange tribute to be the most moving I'd ever observed. A quick look at Adam told me we would need to redo his makeup. He'd smeared it silly by wiping tears from his face.

The Martinezes' pastor stepped up to finish the service. "I can't possibly add anything to that," he said with a smile. "But I would like to read a poem that Marvin loved. In fact, he kept a framed copy on his desk. I think it's appropriate today." He cleared his throat and took a piece of paper from inside his Bible. "As I stumble through this life," he read, "help me to create more laughter than tears, dispense more cheer than gloom, spread more joy than despair. Never let me become so indifferent that I will fail to see the wonder in the eyes of a child, or the twinkle in the eyes of the aged. Never let me forget that my total effort is to cheer people, make them happy, and forget momentarily all the unpleasantness in their lives. And in my final moment, may I hear You whisper, 'When you made My people smile, you made Me smile.'" The minister bowed his head and thanked God for the life Marvin had lived. Then he prayed that God would comfort and protect the Martinez family.

At the last "Amen," Maria got up from her chair and placed a rose on Marvin's casket, the silly red rubber nose still firmly in place on her face. Then she and her two sons, David and Christian, stood near the casket while people offered their condolences. I watched them as I waited for Adam. The idea that Marvin's death might not have been an accident made me feel sick to my stomach. Could it be true? Who would want to hurt him? And who would want to cause his family this kind of pain?

Betty Tuttwiler made her way over to Maria, holding on to her own son's arm. She and Donnie waited behind a couple I didn't know. Suddenly, her eyes narrowed and her expression changed. She was looking at something I couldn't see. Without waiting to speak to Maria, she turned on her heel, pulling Donnie away. She said something to him, and they both walked quickly toward the road where all the cars were parked. I pushed past some of the people around me and hurried over to where she'd stood. There was only one thing out of place—one person who could have caused her odd reaction. Standing against a large tree about two hundred feet away, holding a shovel, stood Clarence Diggs, the groundskeeper. He saw me looking at him and turned around, heading for his nearby truck. He got in, slammed the door, and drove toward a building at the back of the cemetery.

"Was that Mr. Diggs?" Adam had come up behind me.

I grabbed his arm. "Yes," I said keeping my voice low.

"And Betty Tuttwiler knew him, Adam. You should have seen the look on her face."

"That's interesting. The one man we know for certain was here the morning Harold was killed knows his widow?" He turned to look at me. "We need to find out what that's about."

"Yes, we do," I agreed, "but first let's get through Marvin's reception. Betty isn't going anywhere."

"Let's hope Mr. Diggs isn't going anywhere, either."

Billy walked up to us, putting a stop to further discussion. "Great service, wasn't it?"

"Yes, it was," Adam said. "Are you and Mindy ready to go?"

He nodded. "Mindy's already on her way to the car."

With one more look toward Clarence Diggs's truck, now parked in front of the cemetery's maintenance building, Adam led us back down the road.

"I'm afraid we're going to get mud in your car," Adam said as we slopped our way toward the spot where we'd parked.

"Don't worry about it," I said with a smile. "I'll take it to the car wash and have it cleaned inside and out. Those floor mats will look as good as new."

"I guess when you have a cheap car you don't sweat the small stuff as much," Billy said. "I'd make everyone wash their feet before they got inside my pride and joy."

To his credit, Adam just smiled, but when Billy jogged ahead of us to catch up to Mindy, I squeezed his arm. "I like our cars more than his. If he wasn't always shooting his mouth off about the price, you'd never know it was so expensive."

"Shhhh," Adam said with a grin. "I think it's about the only thing his wife doesn't control. She has her own car. Some sporty little red number."

I started to say something else when I noticed Clarence Diggs driving down the access road next to us. If looks could kill, Adam and I would have fallen over dead. We watched him pass us and head for the entrance.

"Wow, did you see that?" I asked.

Adam shrugged. "Well, if he thinks I killed Harold. . ."

"But you didn't," I hissed. "Maybe he's upset because he knows Betty recognized him."

"I don't see how—" Adam's sentence was interrupted by Mindy's high-pitched yelp. We ran as quickly as we could toward my car, with Adam bounding quickly ahead of me. As I neared the spot where Mindy should be, I didn't see her—or her husband. A few other people also hurried over to check on the source of the plaintive scream.

"Oh, for crying out loud!" It was Adam's voice, but where was he? I ran around to the other side of the car and found Mindy sitting in a mud puddle. Billy was on his knees beside her, trying to calm her. Adam, who had bent down to try to help her, stood up with a look of disgust on his face. "It's only a little mud," he said to the hysterical woman. "I thought you were hurt."

Mindy, her clothes spattered with mud and her dyed blond hair wet and dripping, screwed up her otherwise perfect features into something reminiscent of an angry prune, and let loose with another hair-raising screech.

Adam's mouth hung open. He looked like he'd just been told that Watson was actually a funny-looking female poodle. It was obvious he'd never seen an actual adult temper tantrum before.

Billy tried to get her to calm down, but Mindy wasn't paying one bit of attention to him or to the other people standing around looking uncomfortable.

I gently pushed Adam out of the way and bent down next to her. "Oh my goodness, your beautiful dress," I said as kindly as I could. "I'm so sorry, Mindy. What can I do to help you?" I knew I was catering to her, but I'd dealt with this personality type before. Monsieur Max, my first employer, had the very same temperament. I'd come to understand that in his world, as in Mindy's, other people are simply satellites whose only job is to revolve around them.

"Th–this is a designer dress," she sputtered through her tears. "It cost me almost two thousand bucks!"

"It's beautiful," I said soothingly. "I'll bet a good dry cleaner can have it looking as good as new. Let's get you home so you can get it off. I'll help you find someone who can fix it." Actually, I really did know a couple of dry cleaners who could work miracles. I didn't want to explain the reason I knew of them. Sometimes clothing given to funeral homes had stains and needed to be cleaned before it could be placed on the body. I doubted that Mindy would appreciate that story.

"Well. . .okay," she said. "If you promise my dress can be saved." She glared at Billy. "I don't have that many nice dresses. I have to take care of the few good things I have."

Billy knew better than to say anything, but I was pretty sure that beneath his white pancake makeup, his face was beet red. It seemed to me that keeping Mindy happy was a full-time job and that he wasn't always happy about it.

I helped her to her feet. Adam had gotten a blanket out of the back of the Cruiser, and he handed it to me.

"Here, wrap this around you," I said. "We'll take you home."

"Thank you, Hilde," Billy said through clenched teeth. "I'm sorry to cause you all this trouble, but could you possibly drive us back to my car?"

"Sure," I said, "but let's get going. Adam and I still want to go to the reception."

I was pretty sure Billy would have rather gone with us. Unfortunately, it looked like he'd spend the rest of the day catering to his spoiled bride.

Thankfully, we got the couple to their car in record time. I wrote down the numbers of a couple of dry cleaners who had the best chance of returning Mindy's precious designer dress to its original condition. Then we said good-bye to Billy and Mindy.

"Wow," I said to Adam as we pulled onto the highway. "What a couple."

"Billy works harder than anyone I know, so Mindy can have what she wants," he said. "I feel bad for the guy. I don't think she really loves him. She was brought up by rich parents. Her father used to own a large printing company. It went out of business when she was in college, and he had to declare bankruptcy. She had to drop out of school. I don't think she ever got over it."

"How do you know so much about Mindy?"

He smiled. "I went to school with her. In fact, I worked for her dad a couple of summers. Nice man. Died of a heart attack a few years ago. I think it was because of all the stress he dealt with on a daily basis."

"Did you ever date her? I mean, you could have ended up together."

"No, we never dated. I'm afraid Mindy isn't my type."

"And who is your type?" I asked playfully.

"Well, I've always thought Julia Roberts is attractive. . . ."

I slapped him on the arm. "I'll try to get her number. Why don't we send her a picture of you in your clown costume? I bet she'd drop that husband of hers in a second and run to your side."

He laughed and reached over to grab my hand, keeping his other hand on the steering wheel. "If Miss Julia came to my door and threw herself at me, I'd have to tell her, 'Sorry, Julia, but I'm in love with this rather odd young woman with a purple streak in her hair who spends lots of time with dead people.' She'd have to leave brokenhearted."

"I'm beginning to think you have more in common with Mindy than I realized. You're both rather full of yourselves."

He squeezed my hand. "Thank you. Your encouragement keeps me going, you know."

"Very funny. Now put both hands on the steering wheel. Let's talk about what happened at the cemetery."

Adam nodded. "You mean with Clarence Diggs. I've been thinking about it. Maybe she doesn't know him at all. Maybe he just startled her. He is rather odd-looking."

"Why do you say that? Is it that his hair looks like it's never seen a comb? Or could it be his awful mismatched clothes, his missing teeth, or the way he glares at everyone?"

"I would say that none of that helps."

"Well, we've got to find out why Betty reacted the way she did. It might be important."

Adam shrugged. "Maybe we should ask the police to check him out."

"Oh, please. And what will we say? That Harold's wife looked at him funny? We need more than that. They'll just think you're trying to blame someone else to keep yourself out of trouble."

His hands tightened on the steering wheel until his knuckles turned white. "I keep waiting for someone to show up and arrest me. It's not very relaxing."

I put my hand on his shoulder. "They won't arrest you, Adam. They have no proof, and they won't find any. There's nothing linking you to Harold's death except their speculation."

"I know that, but I keep wondering if they'll find something innocent and use it to make me look guilty."

"You've been watching too many crime shows. I don't think the police in Wichita are looking to frame anybody. They're just trying to get to the truth."

"I hope you're right."

"Don't you have any contacts with the department? Seems like you always have clients who can help you."

He nodded. "I do have a couple, but I haven't contacted them. It just doesn't feel right. I wouldn't want to compromise their positions."

I wanted to argue with him, but I knew pushing him to do something he was uncomfortable with was wrong. I would have given several cans of SPAM to know what was happening behind the scenes, though.

Except for reading the written directions to the Christian Lighthouse, the Martinezes' church, we said very little else. I kept turning the situation with Clarence Diggs over in my mind. Diggs was the perfect suspect. He was at the crime scene, he had access to the murder weapon, and he could have committed the murder without anyone seeing him. The only reason he wouldn't be looked at as a suspect was his complete lack of motive. But if he actually knew the Tuttwilers, he could have had a motive to kill Harold. Maybe he was someone the police should look at more seriously.

"Here it is," Adam said, interrupting my thoughts.

We pulled into the parking lot. It was almost full, but

Adam found a spot not too far from the main entrance. We got out and headed toward the door. A handmade sign directed visitors to the room where the Martinez reception was being held.

Although we'd made it through the graveside service without rain, I could smell it in the air. The gathering clouds over our heads promised more moisture. The results of our recent tornado made me feel a little edgy. Suddenly, something else caught my attention, and I forgot about the weather.

"Adam, look," I said, pointing at a car parked close to the entrance. A red Saturn, just like Adam's, sat parked next to a large van with the words CHRISTIAN LIGHTHOUSE painted on its side.

He let go of my hand and walked over to the car. "This is just like mine. Same model, same year."

"We've got to find out who this car belongs to," I said in a low voice, trying to keep a young couple who walked past us from hearing me.

"But Hilde, look around this lot. There are several cars here that look like mine."

I had to agree with him. "But this car is the only one exactly like yours," I said. "We really need to figure out who owns it. If the driver is here for the service, he knew Marvin. And if he knew Marvin, he could have known Harold. We can't walk away from any clue, Adam. There's no way to know what will finally lead us to the real killer."

Adam sighed and ran his hand through his hair. "Okay, but we can't go around questioning all the guests about their cars, and we can't stand out here until someone drives it away. Do you have a plan?"

I looked at the church. "With a little luck, the reception will be on this side of the building. Look at all those windows. Hopefully, while we're inside we'll be able to keep an eye on the parking lot. Let's go in and find out. There's no sense in coming up with a plan B if plan A works."

Adam's eyes narrowed and he grimaced at me. "If you're right, that means that people can see us staring at this car. Doesn't this look a little suspicious?"

"Yes," I said, smiling and nodding. "It certainly does. Get that sour look off your face and smile. Maybe we're just comparing your car to this one. You know, like we think it's cool someone else has a car like yours."

"Yeah, that should work," he said, sarcasm in his voice. "Or we let a killer know that we suspect him. That's always a good thing to do."

I slipped my arm through his and guided him away from the parking lot and toward the building. "Just look innocent. No one will suspect anything."

His fake smile slipped a little. "I am innocent, thank you. I don't have to try to look it."

"I know, I know. It's just that guilty people always look irritated."

Adam stopped dead in his tracks. I almost got whiplash

from his sudden standstill. "So you're telling me that if I'm a little irritated because I've been accused of murder, my car has been impounded, my girlfriend has to drive me around, several of my friends are giving me the fish-eye, and I have no idea if sometime in the next several minutes the cops may swoop in and throw me in jail—people might think I'm a murderer?"

I smiled sweetly at him. "Yes. I think that covers it."

He laughed and shook his head. "You are one of the oddest people I've ever known." He leaned over and kissed me lightly. "I don't know what I'd do without you."

I tugged on his arm. "Well, for one thing, you'd probably stand out in this parking lot until the reception is over. Let's go, Buttercup."

He took a few steps and then stopped again.

"Now what?"

"You know, I'm proud of my clown name. But somehow, having my girlfriend use it. . ."

I grinned up at him. "It threatens your male ego?"

"Yes," he said, his head bobbing up and down with enthusiasm. "I would say it definitely does."

I reached up and pulled his head down to mine and kissed him. "I'm sorry. I'll only call you Buttercup when I really want to bug you. Now move it or lose it."

A nice shove in the middle of his back landed him next to the entrance door, which an elderly gentleman dressed in a black suit opened wide for us. Adam had no other choice but to step inside. I had to wonder if he dreaded this get-together. Although most of the men in Clowns for Christ had expressed their support for him, there were a few who seemed uneasy when he was around. And today there would be other people. Family members and friends of Marvin's and Harold's. I quietly offered a prayer for God's help and protection. It would hurt Adam to think that anyone honestly believed he was capable of murder.

Another man in a dark suit guided us to the hall where the reception was being held. As I suspected, it was the room with all the windows. A quick glance outside gave us a clear view of the other red Saturn. Adam and I made our way over to where Maria and her sons stood. Her red nose was gone now, but my respect for her couldn't have climbed any higher—even if she'd decided to appear in full clown regalia. We offered our condolences to her and her family. I told her how much her comments had meant to me, and she hugged me. When Adam stepped up to her, Maria's eyes got big and she covered a giggle with her hand.

"I think you need some help with your makeup," she said with a grin. "Your face paint has run together."

There were several other outbursts of laughter from people standing around. Adam shot me a dirty look. "Why didn't you tell me?" he asked.

I shrugged. "I'm sorry. I'm just not used to commenting on my boyfriend's makeup." My comment touched off a fresh round of giggles.

Ernie Carson put his hand on Adam's shoulder. "I got a makeup kit with me," he said, grinning. "Why don't you come with me, and we'll get you fixed up."

With Adam telling me he'd be back as soon as he could, I scouted out the food table. I studied the crowd as I munched on a chicken salad sandwich. There were quite a few people in the room I didn't know. Some of them were probably from the church. A lot of the clowns were in attendance, along with their wives. I noticed that a few of them had changed clothes before coming to the reception, while others had only removed parts of their costume. I wondered if Adam had wanted to change, too, but hadn't mentioned it because we were using my car. I felt a little guilty for not thinking to ask him.

I scanned the room for Betty Tuttwiler, but I couldn't locate her. I wasn't surprised. I really hadn't expected to see her at the funeral today after losing her husband only three days earlier. I found it touching that she'd put her own grief on hold to support her friend in her time of need. It was no secret that the Tuttwilers and the Martinez family were close. There was no doubt in my mind that Maria and her children would be front and center at Harold's service.

"I guess I shouldn't be hungry, but everything looks so good." Christian Martinez stood next to me at the buffet table. I introduced myself.

"Oh yes. Adam's friend." He smiled and held out his hand. "My father was so happy Adam finally found someone like you. He's such a great guy. We used to hang out at some of the different events Dad was involved in." He laughed lightly. "Adam was about the only guy close to my age."

"Yes, I've noticed most of the members are. . .well, up there a bit."

He nodded. "I think it's because after men retire, they tend to look for a challenge—something to make life worthwhile." He picked up a pimento cheese sandwich on a small paper plate. "But Adam. . .he just loves making children happy. I've never known anyone quite like him."

"I want you to know how sorry I am about your dad," I said gently. "He was a very special person, too."

"Yes, he was that." Christian stared at the food on the table, but I could tell his mind was somewhere else. His face flushed. "You know, my dad shouldn't have been working by himself in that house. Especially with something electrical. He knew better. The group has renovated a lot of homes for people who needed help. Over the years they've set up certain rules, and one of them is that there's always supposed to be at least two people working together inside these old houses. It's safer that way."

I took his arm and guided him toward the chips and pickles. A line had started to form behind us. "Do you know why he was alone, Christian?" I asked. "Was someone else scheduled to be with him?"

He shook his head. "I don't know. Terry Nicholson was in charge of setting up the work orders, and he was the only one who'd even been inside that place when he did the estimate. I guess he decided it would be safe. Some of the houses the clowns work on are in pretty bad neighborhoods, but not this one." He turned to look at me with tears in his eyes. "If someone else had just checked the breakers, Dad would still be alive." He blinked several times. "I'm not blaming anyone, really. My father could have easily decided to go there on his own. He was pretty independent."

"Maybe someone else *was* supposed to be there, but they didn't show up."

Christian sighed. "I want to ask. I want to find out what went wrong, but this isn't the time for it. I don't doubt that all these guys loved my dad. If one of them messed up, they're probably feeling awful about it. I have doubts as to whether or not I ought to add to their grief. It won't bring my dad back."

"And if your dad did go in alone, without waiting for help?"

Christian put some chips and a pickle spear on his plate and then turned to look at me. My heart almost broke when I saw the sadness on his face. "It would be hard for me to accept. My dad was a smart man. I can hardly believe he would do something so stupid and dangerous."

I picked up my plate and led Christian away from the buffet. We made our way over to the side of the room where there was an empty table with chairs. I motioned for him to sit down.

"Listen, Christian," I said after I took a seat next to him, "your father wasn't the kind of man who would do anything to hurt you or your mother. I may not have known him well, but one thing I did see was his pride in you. He was always talking about you and showing us pictures. He loved to tell everyone that you graduated summa cum laude from college and that you're in the top of your class in medical school."

Christian ran his hand through his short, dark hair, his almost black eyes full of pain. "I know he was proud of me."

"My point is that there is no way he would have put himself into an unsafe situation on purpose. He cared too much about all of you." I put my hand on his arm. "Don't be mad at him."

He stared down at his plate. "Maybe I'm a little mad at God, too. Why didn't He protect him? Why didn't He save my father?"

"Those are questions I can't answer, but I know that it wasn't God's will for your dad to die like that. He loved him—and you. Maybe God did try to warn him. Sometimes we get feelings about things—but we don't listen."

He let out a small laugh. "Now that sounds like Dad. Pushing ahead when he shouldn't. He was a pretty bull-headed guy."

"So bullheaded that he wanted to make sure those kids got their house?"

This time his smile was genuine. "Yes, just that bullheaded."

"One of these days, you'll be able to talk to him about all

this yourself," I said with a smile. "God's got him now, and he's happy. I know that's hard to concentrate on when you're feeling loss, but one of these days, it will mean more to you. In fact, it will mean everything."

He reached over and hugged me. "Thanks, Hilde. Adam's a lucky guy."

Just then, an elderly couple who obviously knew Christian came up to the table and sat down. I finished my sandwich and headed back toward the dessert part of the buffet table. I was just reaching for a piece of banana cream pie when I spotted Betty sitting in the corner of the room, partially hidden behind a piano. She was talking to someone. At first I thought it was her son, but then I realized it was Terry Nicholson, the man who owned the hardware supply business. He appeared to be offering his condolences, but I noticed that he held Betty's hand a little longer than was necessary. I looked around the room but didn't see Terry's wife anywhere. Finally, after a few minutes, he leaned down and kissed Betty on the cheek. Then he walked away.

I looked toward the hallway door where Adam had disappeared. I felt a little odd approaching Betty without him, but if she'd heard that he'd been questioned about Harold's death, it might be better for me to talk to her by myself. I put the plate of pie back on the table and went over to where she sat, grabbing an empty folding chair and bringing it with me. When Betty glanced up and saw me coming, I almost changed my mind. The look she gave me could have frozen lava. After a brief hesitation, I decided to push on.

"Can I get you something, Betty?" I asked as I scooted the chair next to her. "A cup of coffee, something to eat?"

"No, thank you," she said sharply. "I don't need anything from you."

"I'm so sorry about Harold," I said gently, as I eased into my chair. "He was such a wonderful man. He went out of his way to make me feel welcome. I will never forget it."

Betty rubbed her thin hands together, refusing to look at me or acknowledge my presence. I decided there was nothing else I could do but call attention to the elephant in the room.

"Betty, surely you realize that Adam had nothing to do with Harold's death. Adam loved him. Besides, Adam wouldn't hurt anyone. You do know that, don't you?"

She raised her eyes to mine. Anger sparked in them. "No, Hilde. I don't know that. Something was bothering my husband. Something he wouldn't share with me." Her voice broke as she fought her emotions. "All he would say is that someone in the group had done something illegal."

"Did he say it was Adam?"

She hesitated for a moment, looking down at her hands. "Well, no. But he did say he had to talk to Adam. That it couldn't wait another day. That was the morning of his death."

I reached over and took her hand. "But you don't know what he wanted to talk to him about, Betty. It could have been anything."

She pulled her hand away. "If the police suspect Adam,

there must be a reason."

"If they actually had something on him, they would have arrested him, wouldn't they?" I asked. "The only reason they suspect him is because Adam's name was written in Harold's appointment book. It could have meant anything. It certainly doesn't make Adam a cold-blooded killer."

"Harold did have a habit of writing people's names in his book if he wanted to remember to tell them something," she said with a frown. "I used to tell him that the book was for appointments, but he didn't listen to me. He used it for everything."

A thought occurred to me. "Have the police mentioned Adam as a suspect to you?"

Betty shook her head. "No, not really. They did ask questions about him—what Harold's relationship was with him."

"Then why do you think they suspect him?"

For the first time she looked a little uncertain. "I—I heard it from someone else."

"Someone in the clown group?"

She nodded. "I was told they impounded his car."

"Yes, they did. But they haven't found anything. If they had, he would be in jail." I reached for her hand again. This time she didn't pull it back. "You know, I'm the first one to admit that I have some trust issues. To be honest, at first I also wondered if Adam had been involved in some way. But then I really thought about it. You have to know in your heart, like I do in mine, that Adam isn't a killer. It doesn't make sense. Even if you look at it logically, there's no reason for Adam to kill one of his closest friends."

"If you'd seen the look on Harold's face when he said he had to talk to Adam. . ." She hesitated a moment.

"Did he look angry?"

"Well, he certainly looked upset," she said slowly. "I hadn't thought about it until now, but he also looked, I don't know, sad. I asked him if something was wrong, but he wouldn't tell me."

It was a pretty sure bet Harold had realized that he'd accused Adam wrongly of stealing his investment money, and he felt the need to apologize. I wanted to ask Betty about the increase in life insurance Ernie had told us about, but I couldn't think of a way to mention it without sounding like I suspected her.

"Listen, Betty," I said softly. "I'd like to ask you a couple of questions. One of the reasons the police suspect Adam has to do with his car. Someone said they saw it at the cemetery around the time Harold was killed."

Betty let out her breath slowly, and an odd look crossed her face. "Who said that?"

"That's what I wanted to talk to you about. It was Clarence Diggs, the groundskeeper at Shady Rest."

"Clarence Diggs? That's why they tied Adam to my husband's murder?" Hearing Diggs's name clearly upset her. "That man isn't a reliable witness. That's ridiculous."

"Do you know Mr. Diggs?"

"Yes. Many years ago he worked for Harold in his furniture store. A very unpleasant man. Harold eventually had to fire him. He couldn't keep orders straight. Always sending the wrong furniture to the wrong people. My husband tried to help him, but he finally gave up." She shook her head. "When Harold finally had to let him go, Diggs threatened him. Told him he'd get what was coming to him someday."

It felt like my heart jumped into my throat. Diggs had actually tried to intimidate Harold. That made him an excellent suspect. "Did you tell the police about that?"

Betty gave me a look of pity. "That was over twenty years ago, Hilde. I doubt seriously Diggs waited that long to take his revenge. Besides, he actually looked Harold up a few years after he left the store and apologized for what he'd said. He admitted to having a problem with alcohol during the time he worked for us. He'd enrolled in some program that encouraged him to make amends to anyone adversely affected by his habit. Harold accepted his apology. Even helped him buy furniture. They stayed on friendly terms after that, although Harold kept Diggs at a distance. Never did trust him completely." She sighed. "I never liked him. He gave me the creeps. Still does. The last time I saw him was a couple of years ago, after a rather serious fire at the store. Diggs showed up. Said he read about it in the paper and wanted to know if he could help. I encouraged Harold to send him away. We had too much to deal with to keep an eye on him, too." She squeezed my hand. "Of course I'll tell the police about their relationship if you want me to, but I truly think you're barking up the wrong tree."

She gently pulled her hand from mine and signaled to her son, Donnie, who was talking to someone across the room. "I really need to go home. This day has been very difficult. I felt I had to come to support Maria. Harold would have wanted me to." She picked up her purse and stood to her feet. "I'm glad we talked, Hilde. I guess I wanted somewhere to direct my anger. Adam was the only person mentioned to me as a suspect, so I focused on him." She shook her head. "For the life of me, I can't imagine anyone who would want to see Harold dead. He was such a good man." Her thin body trembled with emotion. "You know what? He'd been after me to increase our life insurance for months. I actually argued with him about it. I finally gave in a few weeks ago." She smiled sadly. "You see, even after he's gone, he's still taking care of me. Why would anyone kill a man like that?"

Donnie stepped up and took her arm. "I think it's time you got some rest, Mom," he said gently.

She'd started to walk away when something popped into my mind. "Betty, do you mind if I ask you one other question?"

She turned around. "What is it, Hilde?"

"Why was Harold wearing his costume that morning? I mean, the funeral wasn't scheduled until later in the afternoon."

"He was supposed to go to our granddaughter's school at nine o'clock. Harold was Jessica's guest for show-and-tell. She was proud of her grandpa—and so was I."

She walked away, her steps a little unsteady, her son keeping a tight grip on her arm. I couldn't help but respect her strength. My eyes flushed with tears.

"Oh, great. I'm gone a few minutes, and when I come back, you're crying." Adam appeared next to me, his makeup fixed.

I quickly recounted my conversation with Betty. At first, he was upset that I'd approached her alone, but when I told him about her attitude toward him at first and how it changed, he relaxed.

"Wow. I'm glad she doesn't suspect me now. I can't believe she really thought I'd murder Harold."

I patted his arm. "She's in pain, Adam. She isn't thinking clearly. Forget it." I shook my head. "I'm not sure where we stand. Clarence Diggs knew Harold—even threatened him at one time. But according to Betty, he has no reason to want to hurt him now."

Adam pointed toward the windows in back of us. "I guess you can add this little tidbit to our clues that seem to go nowhere."

I turned around to see Betty and her son get into their car and drive away.

In the red Saturn.

CHAPTER THIRTEEN

After the reception, I took Adam home to change clothes. I wanted to delve a little deeper into Betty's comments but decided to wait. Adam was rather quiet in the car. I suspected he was worn out—not only from his clown duties, but from the emotional roller coaster he'd been on all week.

Before I dropped him off, we called Gabe and made arrangements to meet at his place for dinner so we could talk over the events of the day. While I was at the reception, Paula had called and left a message about a job. It was almost two by the time I pulled into Willowbrook's parking lot. Another service was just getting out. I felt confident there weren't any clowns involved.

To avoid the mourners, I went around to the back door. Paula had left it unlocked for me. Her office was empty. I assumed she was up front, working the current service. I poured a cup of coffee from her pot, which was always on, and waited. About twenty minutes later, she swung her door open.

"Sorry. Things took a little longer than I'd planned." Her

hair color, which she changed whenever the mood hit her, was back to her natural chestnut brown.

"Your hair looks great. What happened? Did Gus finally force you to choose a color actually seen in nature?"

She stuck her tongue out at me. "No, he had nothing to do with it. It might interest you to know that the only time he criticized my hair was when I went green."

I laughed. "I thought that shade came and went rather rapidly. But why the risky step toward normalcy?"

She shrugged and opened a small refrigerator she kept in her office, pulling out a bottle of water. Paula was a water-holic. I'd teased her more than once that her obsession came from watching a movie once where people infected by some kind of strange malady dried up like mummies and died. She'd tried to tell me all the gory details, but I'd stopped her. Those images weren't anything I wanted in my head.

"I figured it was time to find out if I could be happy being lost in a crowd instead of sticking out like a sore thumb."

"You will never get lost in any crowd, Paula," I said. "You're way too pretty. And you know, your natural shade really brings out your eyes. Maybe God had your color scheme figured out right in the first place."

"Let's not get carried away," she said with a grin. "We don't actually know what my real hair color is anymore. This is just a guess. It will take a few months for me to figure out if I've got it right."

"Well, I think you look beautiful."

"Thanks, but you can quit buttering me up. I already like you, and you know I don't have any money."

"Yes, I do know that. I also know you have no sense of loyalty whatsoever, running out on me during the Martinez service like that," I said with a grin. "With all your experience, I assumed you'd be a little more professional."

She came over and plopped down on the couch next to me. "You would think so, wouldn't you?" She put her head back and stared at the ceiling. "It was very sweet. Really. The dedication to helping others, the love people had for him. . ." She giggled and shook her head. "But watching a eulogy given by a guy in makeup with a goofy flowered hat and baggy checked pants was just too much for me. I mean, there are limits. By the way, we got a call from Harold Tuttwiler's family today. They want us to handle his services as well. Thankfully, there won't be any clowns this time. I breathed a big sigh of relief after I got off the phone."

I laughed. "I'm sure that *was* a nice surprise."

"Yes, it was." She sat up straight and smiled at me. "And I'm about to give you an even bigger surprise."

"Uh-oh. Surprises in a funeral home are almost never good."

She patted my shoulder and got up. She walked over to her desk and leaned against it. "Actually, this has nothing to do with Willowbrook. It has to do with our conversation at DeFazio's."

"You mean the one where you reamed me out about Adam?"

"Yes, that one." She raised one eyebrow. "And did you take care of that situation?"

"We've worked it all out. Everything's fine. And thanks."

Paula shrugged. "I just told you the truth. . .like you did for me."

I leaned back and folded my arms. "So what's the surprise?"

She cleared her throat nervously. "I–I'd like to go to church with you on Sunday. If you don't mind."

I could feel tears forming in my eyes. I quickly lowered my head so she wouldn't notice. Getting too demonstrative could scare her off. "Sure, Paula. That would be great."

"I need you to understand that I'm not making any kind of commitment or anything. I still think most Christians act like they think they're better than everyone else, and I'm not interested in that." She smiled at the look on my face. "No, I don't think *you're* that way." She stared down at her shoes. "Just don't expect much, okay? I have a long way to go before I turn into some kind of praise-the-Lord Holy Roller." She raised her head to look at me, her expression serious. "I want you to know that I'm willing to find out just what you see in this God thing. And it's because I see so much love in you, Hilde. No matter how weird I get or what stupid thing I do, you never quit being my friend. If you learned that from God, then I've got to check Him out."

"I understand," I said. "I won't push you." I couldn't hold back a tear that slid down my cheek. "I'm sorry," I said, wiping it away. "I don't know why I'm feeling so emotional.

It's not you, really. It's just that the last few days have been really strange."

Paula laughed. "Well, let's see. Two people you know have died. Your boyfriend's been accused of murder, you've survived a tornado, your long-lost father shows up, and you've had to sit through a clown funeral. I think you're due a few tears. I'd probably have to be locked up."

I grabbed a tissue from my purse, wiped my eyes, and tossed the tissue in the trash. "I'm done—at least for now. I assume you didn't ask me to come here just so I could have a slight emotional breakdown. Is there something else?"

"Actually, there is. Myrna Harcross. She needs your help. Not long before she passed away, a well-intentioned aide who works at her nursing home decided to give her a perm. Let's just say that poor Myrna was caught dead with hair she wouldn't have wanted to be. . ."

"Caught dead with? Lead the way, and I'll see what can be done for Miss Myrna."

I picked up my supply satchel and followed Paula back to where my client waited. Within forty minutes, Myrna looked gorgeous, all signs of the disastrous perm gone.

"Great job, Hilde," Paula said after checking out my work. "Her family will be very relieved."

"That's what it's all about." I packed up my supplies and checked my watch. "Gotta run. I'm making dinner tonight for Gabe and Adam. It's a new recipe."

"I take it your favorite meat product will be the main course?"

I nodded. "I do cook other things, you know. In fact, Adam loves my baked chicken and dressing. But I'm getting ready for the fair, so I'm using Gabe and Adam as human guinea pigs." I winked at her. "I may even enlist your help. Maybe after church Sunday you could come over and try out a few new dishes."

"I'd love to, but I've got to go to my folks' house. Can I take a rain check?"

I closed the fasteners on my satchel. "I can't remember the last time I heard you say you'd made plans with your parents. Your idea or theirs?"

"Mine." She shook her head. "I realized I hurt their feelings by blowing off dinner the other night. I'm trying to be a better daughter, although I have my doubts we'll ever have a normal relationship." She sighed deeply. "But at least spending some time with them on Sunday will help get rid of the guilt I'm feeling."

I reached over and gave her a hug. "Well, it's a step in the right direction. I hope someday you'll actually enjoy being around them."

She rolled her eyes. "Let's not get carried away here, okay?" She held the door open. "You'd better get going. I know that handsome man of yours won't want you to show up late."

I picked up my satchel and my purse and left Willow-brook. I was elated that Paula was going to church with me Sunday, but entering into a relationship with God took more than sitting in a pew. At least Paula would be in the perfect place to learn about Him. I planned to pray really hard that her heart would be open and God would be able to break through the barriers she'd erected.

I went to the store and bought everything I needed for dinner. The checkers knew me and always teased me about buying lots of SPAM products. In the last few months, though, the ribbing had slowed some. Sales of SPAM were soaring. People were discovering it again due to the exorbitant prices of other meat. Today, one of the cashiers asked me for some of my recipes. After getting her e-mail address, I promised to send her a few. Another cashier seemed interested, too.

I called Adam on my cell phone and then drove to his house to pick him up. We got to Eden around four-thirty. Mrs. Hudson and Ida Mae were sitting on the front porch, watching the men from the roofing company work on Ida Mae's roof.

"Doesn't look like they've made much progress," I said to Adam as we came up the steps.

"That's what I think," Mrs. Hudson said. "They've been at it all day, and it looks about the same."

"Now, Arabella," Ida Mae said, "they can't just throw a roof together lickety-split. I'm sure there's lots of structural work to be done first. It looks to me like that's what they're doing now."

Mrs. Hudson clucked her tongue a few times. "Maybe you're right, but I don't want anyone trying to rip you off." She patted her friend's shoulder. "You've been through enough."

Ida Mae laughed. "I doubt if someone who's donating their work can actually 'rip you off,' but thank you anyway." She winked at Adam and me. "Frankly, I'm not willing to look a gift horse in the mouth. I can hardly believe people care anything about an old widow woman like me. It's amazing."

"Not that amazing," I said. "You're a very easy person to love. I'm sure everyone counts it as a privilege to help you."

She waved her hand at me. "You'd better stop it, or you'll have an old *weepy* widow woman on your hands."

"I'm sorry we got back so late," I said. "I got called to a job, and Adam didn't have a way to get here on his own. We're ready to work, though."

Ida Mae shook her head. "All our volunteers left earlier this afternoon. The only people working right now are the professionals. They said they didn't need any assistance with what they're doing, but they would definitely need help tomorrow. Everyone will be back in the morning. You and Adam take the night off and rest. You've been working yourselves silly."

I smiled at her and held the door open for Adam, whose arms were full of groceries. "Well, we did plan to have dinner with Gabe later tonight. Maybe we'll go over a little early."

"That's a good idea. The three of us are planning to sit here in the coolness of the evening and do absolutely nothing but talk and enjoy each other's company."

"Sounds great," I said with a smile. "I need to make some

dinner, Mrs. Hudson. Adam's going to wait and help me carry it across the street."

"That's fine. Just. . ."

"Keep the door open. I know, I know," Adam said with a lopsided grin on his face.

We could hear the women laughing as we trudged up the steps. I was grateful Watson was staying at Gabe's. We usually had to carry him up the stairs because it was difficult for him to make it up without assistance. Trying to carry him, my satchel, and the groceries would have been a chore.

We finally made it to my apartment, got the door open, and put the groceries inside my apartment. I greeted Sherlock while Adam unloaded everything.

He fixed us both a glass of iced tea and sat down in my breakfast nook while I began dinner preparations. I was working on several different dishes for the SPAM recipe contest at the state fair. The first was a dip with cream cheese and red pepper. Then there was the main course, a casserole with a sharp cheddar cheese sauce and noodles. I'd been trying to incorporate different vegetables in it, but hadn't found the perfect combination yet. Broccoli was good, but that had been done to death. This time I was trying cauliflower. I'd been having minimal success with a muffin recipe, but I hoped tonight might yield better results. Cheese biscuits with chopped SPAM Classic had turned out rather well—with the addition of corn and green pepper. I hoped they would be a hit tonight.

"So let's go over your conversation with Betty now," Adam said. "I'm not sure it helped us much. According to you, Betty pretty much ruled out Clarence Diggs as a suspect."

I pulled two cans of SPAM Classic and a can of SPAM Hot & Spicy out of my cupboard. I wanted to try the spicy variety in the dip. It would probably give it just the kick I wanted. "Not necessarily. I know their relationship was a long time ago, but Diggs could still be holding a grudge. Maybe he saw Harold at the gravesite Monday morning, recognized him, and lost it. Or maybe he said something to Harold, started an argument, and picked up that shovel in anger."

"Well, possibly," Adam said slowly. "But that seems pretty far-fetched to me."

I popped the top on one of the cans and sighed with exasperation. "Is it easier to believe you did it?"

"Of course not," he snapped. "I'm just not sure how good a lead this is."

I turned the can upside down and the meat slid out into my bowl. "Basically, it's all we've got. Supposedly everyone loved Harold. There was no reason for anyone to murder him."

"Except his wife," Adam said softly. He held up one hand. "Now I know you said you couldn't believe Betty could kill Harold, but I think we need to look at it, Hilde."

I put all the ingredients for the dip into the bowl and stirred them together. "Betty brought up the increase in their life insurance. If she's telling the truth, it was all his idea."

"But we don't know that for sure. What about her car?"

"You're right," I agreed, "we don't know for certain that she's being honest." I got the plastic wrap out of the cupboard, covered the bowl, and put it in the refrigerator. My compassion for Betty fought a brief battle with my determination to find the truth. "The car could be a coincidence. Besides," I said, after I licked the spoon from the dip, "I've been thinking about how far Diggs was from the gravesite when he says he saw your car."

Adam shrugged. "I don't think he said. I hadn't really thought about it."

I pointed the spoon at him. "He said he saw your car when he came into work. That means he had to have been on the road that leads to the maintenance building. If he drove directly into the cemetery and headed for that building, he would have had a tough time seeing any car parked near Marvin's burial site. The road's on the far side of the cemetery. It doesn't go near Marvin's grave."

"What if he took the road closer to the gravesite?"

"That's possible, but why would he do that? It's not a straight shot from the highway like the other one is. It doesn't make sense. Why would he drive out of his way?"

"I—I don't know," Adam said, staring at me, "but if he really was on the other side of the cemetery, then you're right. He couldn't possibly know for sure it was my car he saw."

I pulled a dish out of the cupboard and started gathering ingredients for my casserole. "That's right. The only thing he could be certain about is that he saw a red car."

"So we start looking for red cars," Adam said glumly. "I think about half the guys in Clowns for Christ have red cars. It's kind of a popular color for clowns."

Something I'd almost forgotten popped into my mind. "How close is Betty to Terry Nicholson?"

He looked puzzled. "I don't know. I mean, Terry's been with the group for a while. Not as long as Harold, but they've probably been friends around five or six years."

"Close friends?"

"I don't really know, Hilde. Anything's possible. Why?"

"Probably nothing. It's just that I saw him talking to Betty at the service."

Adam laughed. "I don't think there's a law against talking to someone. He was probably extending his condolences."

I turned around and leaned against the counter. "You're probably right. His demeanor seemed a little odd, though. He was pretty friendly, holding her hand and kissing her on the cheek."

Adam laughed. "Are you trying to pair Terry and Betty? You think they're having an affair? Goodness gracious, Hilde. Terry's in his fifties—with a wife and family. And Betty, although she's an attractive woman, must be in her early sixties."

"I know. But we have to take the information Albert gave you seriously. It could be important."

"What information?"

"Remember that Albert said he heard them fighting. And that Betty said something about Harold not telling the truth."

Adam thought for a moment. "I'd actually forgotten about that."

I sighed. "It won't do us much good if we don't know what the fight was about. I can't see asking Betty about it now."

"I know you don't like it when I bring up the police, but maybe we should let them question Betty."

His suggestion made me uneasy. "I'm not convinced we have enough evidence yet."

"I know. But Hilde," he said, "like Gabe said, we're not really detectives. At some point, we plan to take everything we've found out to them anyway. Maybe it's time to let them do their jobs."

"That would make a lot more sense if these clues came from someone other than their main suspect." I scowled at him. "Besides, that's exactly what the killer always does, you know. Volunteers information to the police."

"Oh, really. And where did you learn that, Miss Marple?"

I took a large pot out of my cabinet, filled it with water, and put it on the stove. "Goodness, Adam. Everyone knows that. Haven't you ever watched *Columbo*?"

"*Columbo*?" Adam laughed and shook his head. "You mean that old detective show? I guess I have. Why?"

"Whenever someone starts offering to help him solve

the murder, they become his number one suspect." I turned the burner on and started searching for my bag of noodles. "From watching *Columbo,* I learned to never help the police solve a crime, never offer suggestions as to how the murder might have happened, and never get too friendly with them."

Adam leaned back in my breakfast nook, crossed his arms, and with a smirk on his face asked, "And how often have you actually been able to use this wisdom you gleaned from *Columbo*?"

I bent down to look on my lower shelves for the missing bag of noodles. I finally found it hidden behind a can of refried beans. "Okay. Never," I said, standing up straight. "Until now."

Adam grunted. "So let me see if I've got this straight. We're working as hard as we can to find evidence that will exonerate me, but we can't give it to the police because it'll only make me look even more guilty. Does that actually make sense to you?"

I opened the refrigerator and took out a bag of shredded cheddar cheese. "Of course it does."

"Oh, it does? Then what, pray tell, do you plan to do with all this information?"

I swirled around and stared at him. "Did you just say 'pray tell'?"

"I think I did. It felt like a 'pray tell' moment."

"I see. I've never heard of a 'pray tell' moment. I wasn't aware they existed."

"Obviously you were wrong."

"Obviously."

"So your answer is?" Adam said, his voice a little higher than it should be.

"My answer to what?"

He put his head down on the table while I found a pan for the cheese sauce. He mumbled something but I couldn't hear him.

"You'll have to speak up."

He raised his head and looked at me strangely. "I said, I'm going to prison. Could you start working on a SPAM cake? Maybe find a way to stick a file in it?"

I shook my head. "I wouldn't ruin a good recipe with a dirty file. Besides, this isn't the fifties. I don't think a file will help you break out of jail anymore. Everything's electronic."

He blew his breath out slowly, never taking his eyes off me. "You're an odd and wonderful woman. You know that, right?"

"Yes, I do." I poured some milk into the pan and turned the burner on. "Now keep an eye on this milk while I change."

He scooted out of the nook and stood in front of the stove. "Into who?"

"Very funny."

I grabbed some jeans and a sweatshirt from my closet and went to the bathroom to get out of my funeral dress. I call it that because it's my only black dress. I wear it to every funeral I attend. I figure the guest of honor will never know.

For a dress, it's not half bad.

While I was changing, my thoughts turned back to my discussion with Adam. Although I'd been teasing, he'd actually brought up a good point. What were we going to do with our suspicions? It wasn't that I hadn't thought of it, but I guess I'd been concentrating so much on the problem, I hadn't quite figured out what to do with the solution.

I finished dressing and went back to my apartment. Adam was staring at the pan of milk with a panicked look on his face. "You didn't say exactly what I'm supposed to be watching for," he said accusingly. "It started to boil so I turned it down."

"You did just the right thing." I hung up my dress and put my slip in the dresser drawer. A look at my poor leather boots told me that it was definitely time to say good-bye. I dug around in the back of my closet and found an old pair of black sneakers. They'd have to do until I could buy some new boots.

"I'm so relieved," Adam said. "This is starting to look pretty good. I'm starving. I didn't get a bite at the reception."

He scooted back into the booth while I put all the ingredients in the pan of hot milk. "We'll ask Gabe what to do with our evidence. He's always got good advice."

"And why is that?" Adam asked, shaking his head. "I've never met anyone like him. He seems to know something about everything. I swear, sometimes he talks like a detective. He probably even understands your *Columbo* thing."

I nodded while I stirred. "I know. But like I told you before, his past is off-limits."

"I'm not planning to say anything, but it sure is weird."

He got up and walked over to the front windows. After commenting about how far along the work on Ida Mae's roof had progressed, he sat down and promptly dozed off. I let him sleep while I finished getting the food ready. When it was done, I packed it into my large wooden picnic basket. Then I reluctantly woke him. After getting his bearings, he picked up the basket and we started toward Gabe's. Outside, Mrs. Hudson's insurance man was just getting ready to leave.

"Hello there, Miss Higgins," he greeted me. "And Mr. Sawyer."

Adam stuck out his free hand. "Good to see you, Mr. Goetz. How are things going?"

Goetz. That was it. Adam shook his hand heartily.

"Just fine. Everything is progressing nicely. I was here earlier today to give Mrs. Hudson an update. I came back by this evening to drop off some paperwork I forgot." He clapped his hands together and smiled broadly. "I hope to have her fixed up before long." He turned his happy face toward me. "Work on the garage begins tomorrow. We should have a nice place for your car by the end of next week."

I smiled. "Thank you, Mr. Goetz. I can hardly wait."

Adam and I said good-bye and had just started to cross the road when Goetz called out my name. "Oh, Miss Higgins. That man came by again this morning."

"I'm sorry," I said, looking back at him. "What man are you talking about?"

"The one looking for his friend. I got the name this time. He's looking for a man named Bastian."

Good thing Adam was holding the basket, or I would have dropped it. "Did you say Bastian?"

The small man nodded his head vigorously. "Yes, that's definitely the name. I wonder if he meant Mr. Bashevis?"

I felt dizzy. "Did—did you mention Mr. Bashevis to this guy?"

"No," he said with a frown. "I didn't think about it until he'd driven away. I'm sorry. Should I have?"

I walked back to him. "No. And please, Mr. Goetz, don't talk to this man if he comes by again. I don't think his intentions are good."

Goetz's eyes grew wide. "Oh dear. I'm sorry. If he tries to speak to me again, I'll just ignore him."

I asked him to describe the man he saw and the car he drove. It was quickly apparent that it was the same car I'd seen the other day, driving slowly through Eden. I'd forgotten Goetz's earlier comment about a man looking for someone with a name similar to Gabe's. The pressure of the last few days had wiped it out of my mind. I could only pray that it wasn't the kind of mistake that can't be fixed—that my absentmindedness wouldn't prove costly to my friend.

I thanked Goetz and went back to where Adam stood waiting.

"What was all that about?"

"Let's get a little farther away before I tell you." I didn't want to make Goetz suspicious, although I doubted he cared much about an old antiques dealer in a town the size of Eden. But there was no reason to take chances. When we were almost across the road, I grabbed Adam's arm. "Some man's been looking for Gabe," I said. "Goetz told me about it a couple of days ago, but I didn't make the connection. I saw this guy drive through Eden the other night."

"My goodness, Hilde. You look terrified. Why are you assuming this man wants to harm Gabe? Maybe it's nothing at all."

"I don't think it's nothing. He used Gabe's real name."

Adam stopped in his tracks and his mouth dropped open. "His real name? What real name?" He frowned at me. "All you ever told me was that Gabe's past was some kind of secret. You never mentioned he was using an alias." He looked toward our friend's house. "I don't know, Hilde. This is beginning to sound. . .well, dangerous."

"Adam, it's Gabe. He's not dangerous and you know it."

He didn't move, just kept staring at the house.

I pulled on his arm. "Hey, Gabe believes in you. Maybe that should go both ways."

Adam took a step forward, but his expression clearly showed his concern. "I don't think it's a matter of not trusting him. It's this man who's been poking around. We have no idea who he is, what he wants, or what his intentions are. I—I don't want you involved in something that could hurt you."

I stood on my tiptoes and kissed him. "Thank you, but I'm not a child. Nor do I need your protection. But it means a lot to me that you want to keep me safe."

I joined Adam in gazing at the building where Gabriel Bastian waited for us. "There's only one thing we can do, Adam. We have to tell him about the man. What happens after that is up to him."

"What does that mean?"

"I don't really know," I said, unable to keep my voice from breaking. "But I'm afraid he may leave Eden for good."

CHAPTER ⚏⚏ FOURTEEN

I convinced Adam not to blurt out the information about the stranger in Eden as soon as we walked into Gabe's apartment. The camera mounted at the front door, the way he kept to himself, the package he'd received from a hotel in the Ukraine, even his reluctance to pick Adam and me up at the police station; all these things rushed together in my mind to create a scenario that frightened me. Gabe was in some kind of trouble, and the man who'd been patrolling Eden was here to cause it. It all made sense. I knew I had to tell him the truth, but I didn't want to. I was afraid of losing him. He had become my friend. Since Mr. Goetz hadn't told the man where Gabe lived, I didn't feel as if he needed to make an immediate escape. Surely we could have one last dinner in peace before I dropped the bomb.

We made it through our meal, focusing primarily on the dishes I'd made. I'd already told Gabe that I needed his input because I was searching for the recipe I would use at the state fair in September. But I couldn't keep him from noticing that something was on my mind. My mother had always claimed that I could never make it as an actress. My emotions invariably show on my face.

"Hilde," he said as he picked up our dishes and carried them to the sink, "what's on your mind? I can tell something's wrong."

I glanced over at Adam, who nodded his encouragement. Gabe's unusually jovial attitude made me feel even guiltier. I'd never seen him so lighthearted. Now I was getting ready to pull the rug out from under him. "Some very interesting things happened today that pertain to Adam," I said, "but— but that's not what's bothering me right now." I stared at him while trying to find the right words. "Gabe, could you sit down, please?"

He ambled over to the table and slid into his chair. We'd elected to eat in his cozy kitchen. I loved the elegant dining room where the portrait of a woman hung—the same woman whose picture had been inside the package I'd delivered to him so many months ago. But I felt more comfortable in the kitchen, with its gleaming appliances and personal touches. Gabe's charming ceramic teapot sat on the counter, waiting to serve a brand new and exciting tea. A beautifully engraved tin that held cookies and special pastries rested against an old, wooden pepper mill. The cups we'd sipped from so many times hung from hooks under cabinets that held all the plates and dishes we'd used for our dinners. The thought that today might be the last day we would spend this special time together overwhelmed me. I couldn't stop the tears that started to fall down my cheeks.

"For goodness' sakes, Hilde," Gabe said, "what's going on?"

Little by little, between sobs, I got the story out. "M– Mr. Goetz told me about this guy a few days ago," I said. "He—he was looking for s–someone. Someone with a name like yours. B–but I didn't put it together until today when he told me he was searching for a man named Bastian. I saw this guy, too, Gabe, driving through town. It's you he's trying to find. I–I'm sorry I didn't realize sooner that you were in danger. I've been so distracted by everything that's happened. . . ." I picked up my napkin and wiped my face. "Are—are you going to have to leave?"

The look on Gabe's face was unreadable. I couldn't tell if he was shocked, angry, or frightened. Then he did the last thing I expected. He started to laugh loudly, as if I'd just said the most humorous thing he'd ever heard.

Adam looked as confused as I felt. We weren't prepared at all for this kind of reaction. Hopefully, my information hadn't caused him to snap. There was nothing we could do but wait for him to settle down and explain himself. His odd response was unnerving, to say the least. Finally, his guffaws turned to small spurts.

"I'm sorry, Hilde," he said, dabbing at the corners of his eyes. "It's not funny, really. It's just. . ." He reached over and took my hand. "Do you have any idea how blessed I feel to have you and Adam in my life?" He shook his head. "You've brought sunshine back to me. I feel alive again."

"But that man. . ."

He patted my hand. "That man is my brother-in-law. He gave up trying to ask anyone where I lived and started knocking on doors. Since there aren't many houses in Eden, it didn't take him long to find me. He stopped by here after you two left for the funeral this morning. If my sign hadn't blown down, he probably would have found me the first day he came looking for me."

To say I was surprised was an understatement. "Your brother-in-law? For crying out loud—I thought he was a hit man or something."

Gabe raised one eyebrow. "You sound disappointed. Did you want him to be a hit man?"

I scowled at him. "Of course not. Don't be silly."

Adam cleared his throat. "Listen, I know we're not supposed to ask you anything about your life before you came to Eden, but Hilde says your name isn't really Bashevis."

"I'm sorry, Gabe," I said sheepishly. "It just kind of slipped out. I didn't mean to tell him."

"You saw the name on that package you delivered to me a few months ago, didn't you?"

I nodded, feeling miserable. "Yes."

"Don't worry about it, Hilde. It doesn't matter anymore."

"Look, Gabe," Adam interjected. "I don't want to offend you, but. . ."

"What did I do that forced me to change my name and

hide out in Eden?"

"Yeah. I guess I'm a little worried about Hilde. Is she in any danger?"

"No, she's not in danger." He looked at the clock on the kitchen wall. "I'm going to briefly explain what's going on. We'll talk more about it later. In fact, you can ask anything you want to then. But I really think Adam's situation is more important than mine right now. So you must promise that what I tell you now will suffice until we have more time. Is that agreed?"

Adam and I both nodded vigorously.

Gabe got up and filled his teakettle with water. Then he put it on the stove and sat back down. "I wasn't raised in America," he said. "I grew up in England. I know you can't tell it by my accent. Actually, I worked hard to lose it when I came here. I wanted to blend in—to hide out because of problems caused by my profession. You see, after I graduated from a British university, I joined the police force."

"I knew it," I said triumphantly. "I guessed you'd been involved in law enforcement."

"Hilde, this was years ago. Believe me, police procedures today are quite different than what I experienced."

"But you understand the principles."

The kettle began to whistle, and he got up and removed it from the burner. "Yes, I guess that's probably true." He took his ceramic teapot and put several scoops of tea into the infuser ball. Then he poured the hot water over it. "People's motives haven't changed that much, even though investigative techniques have improved considerably."

He put the pot aside so the tea could brew and sat back down at the table. "Anyway, I did fairly well. I was promoted, and eventually I was transferred to a special undercover division that dealt with organized crime. There were some rough groups trying to take over London back then. I helped to put away the leaders of a particularly nasty band of criminals who practically ran the drug trade during those days." Gabe stared up at the ceiling as if he could see the past reflected there. "I met a young woman who was attending art school in London. We fell in love. Mariah's family was from France, and they were quite wealthy. My family was not. Although I had a job with a lot of responsibility and danger, I didn't make much money. Her family opposed our relationship. They wanted her to marry someone worthy of her social status. She disregarded her family's wishes and married me anyway."

"Is she the woman in the painting?" I asked.

He nodded. "Yes. I painted it from memory. She looks the way she did the last time I saw her. She's also the woman whose picture you saw in the package I got from the Ukraine."

I'd never admitted that I'd seen the contents of that envelope, but somehow he'd known.

He sighed and folded his arms over his chest. "I don't want to go into too many details, but back then, there was a man who had a lot of power in London. He basically ran the criminal underground—kind of like a mafia boss. I oversaw an operation that put quite a few of his associates in prison. Two of the men convicted and sent away were his own sons. He swore his revenge against me, but he wasn't content to just kill me. He wanted me to endure the loss of the person who was most important to me. That way, in his mind, I would suffer the way he had. He told me to leave the country and to never see Mariah again. He promised that if I got anywhere near her, he'd know. In fact, he said that if he ever found me, he would kill Mariah first—and then kill me. This was his way of ensuring that I could never go home again." Gabe shook his head. "Although we'd rounded up quite a few members of his gang, there were others. Some of them we knew. Many we did not. There was no way to know who was watching me—and Mariah. This man made it clear that he not only intended to kill my wife, but that he would kidnap and torture her until she begged for death. Then he'd send me pictures of her body." He shrugged. "I had no choice but to believe him. At first, Mariah and I thought we could leave the country together. We'd go somewhere far away where he couldn't find us. But Mariah's family was convinced I couldn't keep her safe. That this man was too powerful for me. For both of us." He smiled sadly. "In the end, out of fear, Mariah allowed them to send her away. They wouldn't tell me where she was, and after a while, I decided they were probably right. That my desire to be with her was destructive to her—and to me."

"So did you ever see her again?" Adam asked.

He shook his head. "No. I came to America. It was the only way I knew to keep her safe. I figured if there was an ocean between us, and neither one of us knew where the other one was, she would be protected." He lifted his hand and made a sweeping gesture. "I bought this place in Eden, the smallest and most forlorn town I could find, set up a failing antiques shop, and hid out. Although my living space is comfortable, I purposely keep the shop in the condition it is so that no one even suspects that anyone but a poor antiques dealer lives here. My cover has held for all these years." He looked at me with a raised eyebrow. "That is, until you started sniffing around. Although my instinct was to send you packing, I just couldn't. I guess loneliness had taken its toll. Of course, I had no idea how nosy you would turn out to be."

"I'm not nosy. I'm just. . .interested," I sniffed.

"No, you're nosy," Adam said, grinning.

I ignored him. "What about Mariah, Gabe? What happened to her?"

He smiled sadly. "For all these years I haven't known if she was alive or dead. And then the packet arrived. It was originally sent to Robert, a friend of mine, by someone in Mariah's family who thought he might know where I was. He did, and he sent the package to me. The picture of Mariah and me that you saw, with the word *murder* written across it, is the same photograph that was sent to me all those years ago as a threat. The picture was taken of us when we had no idea we were being photographed. It was meant to show us how vulnerable we were—that this crime boss could get to us anytime he wanted to. Mariah's family kept it all these years—I guess as a way to remind her that she should stay away from me."

I frowned at him. "Why did Mariah's family contact you now?"

Gabe rubbed his eyes and was silent for a moment. When he looked at us again, there were tears in his eyes. "To let me know that Mariah had died, and that there was no longer any threat. Robert got the picture, along with an explanation, and he sent it to me. He felt I should know she was gone."

"I'm sorry," I said softly. "Are you okay?"

"I will be. Truthfully, I knew this day would come, and I tried to prepare myself for it. Still, hearing the news shook me."

"But one thing I still don't understand. Why did you react so violently when you saw that envelope? I mean, you had no idea what was in the package, right?"

"That's right. It was seeing my real last name. Robert knows the alias I'm living under, but he forgot and wrote 'Bastian' instead of 'Bashevis.' I hadn't seen that name in almost forty years, and the return address was unfamiliar to me. My reaction was simply shock and the long-held fear that someone had found me."

Gabe got up and checked the tea. He must have been satisfied that it had brewed long enough. He took out the filter and carried the pot to the table, pouring Adam and me each a cup. He took a small container from the refrigerator and set it on the table. We knew it meant that he felt this tea tasted better with milk. Learning that Gabe had grown up in England hadn't come as a surprise to me. His propensity for tea and the desserts he served had already clued me in to his roots. But being told I couldn't ask questions had stopped me from confirming my suspicions.

"So you thought that package was from her," I said. "That she'd found you."

"Exactly. Robert sent it to me from a hotel in the Ukraine. He'd been staying there for a couple of months. His mother was ill and he wanted to be near her. I had no idea who would be sending me something from there. My first thought was that it might be Mariah."

"Did you really think she was still in danger after all this time?" Adam asked.

Gabe shrugged. "I couldn't take the chance. This was a very evil man, who prided himself in seeking vengeance against anyone who crossed him. As I said, he had many men working for him. Men who had sworn their unconditional loyalty to him. And his sons could easily be out of prison now. I had no idea if they intended to complete their father's threats of vengeance."

"You said *was*?" I asked.

He nodded. "The man who came to see me is Mariah's younger brother. He's also the person who notified Robert of her death. He traveled all the way to Eden to tell me how sorry he was that his family separated us." Gabe's voice softened. "He felt he needed to talk to me in person—to tell me that Mariah had always loved me. That she had tried to find me, just as I feared she would. She never married again." He rubbed his eyes again and took a deep breath. "He also wanted me to know that this man, the one who ruined our lives, was dead and that his gang had scattered. No one is looking for me or Mariah anymore. We're both free."

"If only he'd died years ago," I said gently, "you and Mariah could have been together again."

Gabe cocked his head sideways and smiled at me. "But we will be together again, Hilde. It's a promise we made to each other long ago. That we would trust God to reunite us someday. I believe with all my heart that He will."

I returned his smile. "I do, too."

Adam still looked puzzled. "Okay, I understand all of that. But why didn't you want to pick Hilde and me up at the police station the other day? Did you really think the police would somehow connect you to this bad guy?"

Gabe's bushy eyebrows shot up with surprise. Then he laughed. "Oh, my goodness, no. I hardly ever drive my truck anymore. I forgot to renew my car tags. They're expired."

I sighed and shook my head. "We thought there was some kind of nefarious reason you didn't want the police to see you."

Gabe grinned. "There was. I was afraid I'd get a ticket."

"So who will you be now?" Adam asked. "Gabe Bashevis or Gabe Bastian?"

"For now I'll keep the name Bashevis," he said. "It would take some effort to change it back. Perhaps someday I will." He refilled our teacups. "Now, if you don't mind, I'd like to change the subject. We'll have plenty of time to talk about me later. Adam's problems seem a little more pressing right now. So tell me about today. Have we learned anything new?"

It was tough changing gears. My mind was still chewing on Gabe's story. I felt a sense of relief. He wasn't leaving—at least for now. I wondered if he might decide to return to England someday. I could only hope that he felt more at home in the United States. He'd been here a long time. I suddenly realized that Gabe and Adam were staring at me.

"Oh, right. Sorry," I said. "About today."

"If you don't mind," Gabe said.

I grinned at him. "Okay, don't get pushy."

I proceeded to tell him everything I'd learned at the reception. About Clarence Diggs, my conversation with Betty, her friendliness with Terry Nicholson, the fact that her car was exactly the same as Adam's, and what Christian Martinez had said about Marvin being in the house alone. "One specific thing Betty said that I found the most interesting," I said, "was that Harold told her someone in the group had done something illegal."

Adam looked alarmed. "She didn't say it was me, did she?"

"No. She had no idea who it was. She did say that Harold said he had to talk to you, though."

"I can't prove it," Gabe said, "but it sounds to me like Harold wanted to apologize to you, Adam." He frowned at me. "Didn't you say that Betty told you Harold wrote people's names in his scheduler for other reasons besides reminding himself of appointments?"

I nodded.

"Then I'll bet that's what it was. He was upset about something someone else had done, and he was sorry he took it out on you, Adam."

"That's exactly what I think," I said.

"I hope you're right," Adam said. "But aren't you both making kind of a big jump?"

"I don't think so," Gabe said with a smile. "Remember Sherlock?"

"My fish?" I interjected.

Gabe sighed and shook his head. "Help me, God. No, not your fish."

"Sorry. I know what you mean. Whatever's impossible. . ."

"Yes. We know that it's impossible Adam murdered Harold."

I smiled at Adam. "Yes. We know that's impossible."

"And we know that Adam didn't steal money from Harold's portfolio. That's impossible, too."

"Yes."

"Then what did Harold want to talk to you about, Adam?

The only thing that could have been weighing on his mind was his argument with you. He knew he was wrong. He had to have figured out that the losses in his account had to do with the stock market, not you. So the only thing left, because Harold was a good, ethical man who cared about people, is that he wanted to tell you he was sorry for accusing you of something he knew you couldn't have done."

"That makes sense," Adam said slowly. "Thanks. I feel better."

I stared at Gabe with my mouth open. "You're a little scary. That's a great deduction."

"You could have easily figured it out," Gabe said. "You have the kind of mind that. . ."

"Excuse me," Adam said, tapping his fingers on the tabletop. "If your mutual admiration society can take a small break, could we get back to finding out who killed Harold?"

"Now, Adam," I said as soothingly as I could, "we think you're smart, too. Don't be jealous."

Adam's right eyebrow shot up so high it disappeared behind the hair that hung down on his forehead. "Thanks so much," he said sarcastically

Gabe grunted. "Adam's right. Back to basics. So Harold is concerned about some kind of illegal activity going on in the group. Unfortunately, that could be almost anything."

"But Harold had an argument with Marvin," I said. "Could it have been him?"

"Well, that doesn't make sense," Adam said. "Marvin was

doing something illegal so he electrocuted himself, came back from the dead, and clunked Harold over the head?"

"You're absolutely right," Gabe said. "That doesn't make any sense." He stared at his teacup, lost in thought. "Let's put the comment about illegal activity on the shelf for now. That may be the *why* of our murder. But the clues will probably lead us to the *who* first. Then the motive should be able to confirm our suspicions."

"Don't we have to assume that Marvin's death was accidental?" Adam asked. "I mean, we have no proof it was anything else. Just because he had an argument with Harold. . . I mean, I had an argument with him, too."

"Exactly. And it's one of the reasons the police will suspect you even more," Gabe said. "Looking into recent personal problems is something investigators do as a matter of procedure. Many times it points to the reason behind a murder."

"But they don't know Adam had a disagreement with him, yet," I said.

Gabe shook his head. "I wouldn't be so sure. Adam, where did this altercation take place?"

"At my office."

"And who else was around?"

Adam thought for a moment. "Actually, we were pretty much alone. Several of our partners are out now. The only person I can think of would be the receptionist, Tammy Sue."

"I can guarantee you that the police have talked to her. Is

there any reason she wouldn't tell the truth if she was asked about your relationship with Harold?"

"No. Tammy Sue and I get along fine, but I wouldn't consider us friends. I mean, we don't see each other outside of work."

"Then we have to assume they know there was some kind of problem between you and their murder victim."

"Then why haven't they arrested him, Gabe?" I asked. "In fact, why haven't we heard anything from them? Is that a good sign?"

"No. It's not a good sign at all. If he were no longer a suspect, they would have notified him. My guess is they're waiting for something more concrete—something to link him directly to the murder. I'm sure they've tested the shovel for fingerprints. If they'd found Adam's, he definitely would have been contacted by now."

"But if they haven't found them, doesn't that clear me?" Adam asked.

"No, not necessarily. The killer could have been wearing gloves. Or the prints may be too smudged to be useful. Not finding your prints still doesn't rule you out."

Adam grunted. "Great. What about my car? When they don't discover anything in it to incriminate me, won't that force them to assume I'm not guilty? I mean, I don't know anything about crime scenes beyond what I see on TV, but hitting someone on the head might cause the killer to get blood on him, right? When they realize there's no blood. . ."

"They'll simply look elsewhere. Not everyone who's charged with murder is found guilty through direct evidence. In fact, there are many cases of people being convicted through circumstantial evidence alone."

"I don't like that," I said. "Should people actually be convicted without some kind of concrete proof that points to them?"

Gabe shrugged. "Personally, I'm terribly uncomfortable with cases built on circumstances alone. I don't think pure conjecture and guesswork should enter into our judicial system. It leaves too much to chance and can turn a case into a personality contest. Reasonable doubt should include the lack of direct evidence."

Adam's complexion had gone pale. "So you're saying that even if there's no proof I killed Harold, I could be sent to prison anyway?"

"No," Gabe said evenly. "I don't mean that at all. But I am saying that I would feel a lot better if we could uncover clear evidence that leads us to the real killer."

"So when do we turn over what we know to the police?" I asked. "Adam thinks we should tell them what we've learned so far, but I'm not convinced. It's like those old *Columbo* shows. . ."

"Where the guilty person does everything they can to assist the police?" Gabe laughed. "I don't think it works quite that way in the real world, but I'd feel more comfortable if we could get something a little more solid than what we have now."

"I knew you'd understand the *Columbo* thing," Adam muttered. He leaned back in his chair and stretched his arms over his head. "Well, if my recent altercation with Harold is important, shouldn't we try to find out what Harold and Marvin argued about? And what about Betty and Harold?"

"You know, Harold seemed to be such a happy, laid-back guy," I said. "We're talking about three different quarrels he had, all within a few days. It sounds to me like he was definitely upset about something."

"As long as I've known him," Adam said, "he's always been easygoing and calm. I mean, he could get upset like anyone else, but for the most part, I'd have to say it took a lot to get him riled."

"Adam," Gabe said, "can you give us a list with the names of everyone in your group and what kind of work they do? If we know the kind of jobs people have, or had if they're retired, it might help us to guess what they might have done that was illegal."

"Sure," Adam said.

"But what if it had nothing to do with their professions?" I asked. "I mean, stealing cable is illegal, but if I did it, it wouldn't have a thing to do with my job."

"I really don't think Harold was killed over stolen cable," Gabe said dryly.

"You know what I mean," I said, shooting Gabe a dirty look. "So what else can we do?"

"I think we need to talk to anyone who might have overheard Harold's spats with Marvin and Betty." Gabe rubbed his hands together. It reminded me of one of the villains in an old-fashioned melodrama. I expected him to say, "Muwahaha," but he didn't. "Something happened," Gabe continued. "Something that changed his usual demeanor. My guess is that if we can find out what it was, we'll find our killer."

"I don't see how we can do that, Gabe," I said, a feeling of frustration building inside me. "Marvin's dead, and I can't ask Betty—not right now."

"Maybe we can," Gabe said. "Where did these arguments occur? Do you remember, Hilde?"

"Well, the quarrel with Marvin happened at the furniture store, and his dispute with Betty happened at the potluck dinner last month."

"We need to question people who might have overhead them. Just like the police probably did at my office," Adam interjected. "Find out if they heard anything that might help."

"Well, yes and no." Gabe reached down to pet Watson, who was snoring contentedly at his feet. "Hilde and I need to talk to them. You can't go around asking these kinds of questions right now since you're under suspicion. You'll have to let us take care of it."

"And what do I do?" Adam asked with a frown.

I reached over and grabbed his hand. "You help Ida Mae. Tomorrow's a big work day. You'll have lots to do."

"Okay, but it sure seems like I should be hanging out with you guys."

"Some of the men who were at the dinner last month will be here tomorrow," I said to Gabe. "Hopefully, Albert will be one of them. He's the one who told me about the argument between Betty and Harold. We can talk to him. Make sure he didn't hear more than he told me. And find out who else might have overheard something."

Gabe nodded. "What about Harold's son? Do you think he'd talk to us?"

I shrugged. "I don't know. I've met him, but that's all."

"Donnie and I went to high school together," Adam said. "And we were both on the track team. He called me the other day to tell me he'd heard the police suspected me and that he knew I had nothing to do with his father's murder. He'll talk to you. But in this case, I think you should let me call him first and let him know why you want to meet with him."

"Okay," Gabe said. "Sounds like a good idea." He looked at the clock on the wall. "Why don't we wrap this up? We could all use some sleep. We'll start fresh in the morning. Hilde and I will start making the rounds." He shook his finger at me. "And that includes Clarence Diggs. We've got to ask him a few questions. I know he doesn't seem like a solid suspect, but he's involved in this. He's the main witness against Adam, and he knew Harold. We've got to dig a little deeper and see if he can tell us something important that we might not know."

"I doubt that he'll be very forthcoming," I said doubtfully. "But we can try."

Gabe grinned. "Mr. Diggs appears to be the kind of person who will cooperate with the right incentive."

"The right incentive? Are you talking about money?" I asked. "Wouldn't that be unethical? I mean, what would the police say?"

"They won't say anything because they won't know."

"Well, maybe *we* won't tell them," Adam said. "But what if Diggs says something?"

"What could he say?" Gabe asked. "If he takes the money, it makes him look like a rather unreliable witness, doesn't it? Maybe we'll get some helpful information—and maybe not. But we've effectively downgraded the power of his testimony with any jury."

"With a jury?" Adam said. His eyes were wide with alarm. "You think this will actually go to trial?"

"No. No, I don't," Gabe said calmly. "I'm just trying to explain that offering Diggs money won't hurt us. It will hurt him more if he takes it."

"It sounds to me like you've done this before," I said.

Gabe's slow smile told me all I needed to know. "Let's just say that Solomon's advice about the effectiveness of a bribe was right on. I'm not saying it's always the best thing to do, but I've seen it loosen the tongues of quite a few witnesses. For the most part, these are individuals who don't care about helping anyone except themselves." He shrugged. "Honest people who place value on right and wrong turn the money down and offer their testimony for nothing. Money has a way of revealing one's true nature."

"The love of money," I said, shaking my head. "It certainly corrupts."

"Yes, it does," Gabe said. "Sometimes. But there are people who can be trusted with financial blessing. I think God searches for them. There's a lot of good that can be done in this world if you look for the right opportunities."

"You mean like helping Mrs. Hudson and Ida Mae?" I said with a smile.

"I'm sure I don't know what you're talking about." Gabe's overly emoted look of innocence made me giggle.

"I'm sure you don't."

He stood up. "Now get out of here, Hilde," he said. "It's time for you to get some sleep."

I gulped down the last of my tea and stood up. "Come on," I said to Adam. "I'll drive you home."

He yawned. "Actually, I'm staying with Gabe again." He pointed to a bag he'd brought with him.

"Well then," I said, "I guess I'll see you both in the morning."

Gabe put his arm around my shoulders. "Why don't you come over for breakfast? I'll cook. I make a mean waffle."

"Sounds great. What time?"

"Not too early," Adam said, yawning again. This time he made me yawn as well.

"How about nine?" Gabe said.

"It's a date." I leaned over and scratched Watson behind the ear. "Why don't Adam and I take this little guy outside? Adam can bring him back upstairs after he's done his doggy duties."

"His doggy duties?" Gabe's eyebrows shot up. "Never heard it said quite that way before, but it sounds like a good idea."

I started to pack up my dishes, but Gabe stopped me. "Leave them, Hilde. You can get them tomorrow. I'll run the dishwasher tonight, and you won't have to worry about them."

"Thanks." I was too tired to argue with him. "Let's go, guys," I said, heading toward the stairs.

Adam called Watson and then picked him up when he scooted out from under the table. I waved good-bye to Gabe, and the three of us went outside. With all the rain we'd had lately, I was almost surprised to find clear skies, littered with sparkling stars.

"Absolutely beautiful," I said, gazing upward.

"Yes, you are," Adam said softly, kissing me. Watson wiggled around in his arms and licked me on the cheek.

I laughed. "I've never been kissed by two guys at the same time. I feel so special."

"You *are* special," Adam said. He put Watson on the ground. The little dog immediately began running around, looking for a place to do his business.

"Thank you. Right now, though, I just feel sleepy." I hugged him and started to step away, but he pulled me back. There was something about the night, the stars, and the feeling of his arms around me that made me feel giddy.

"When this is over," he whispered in my ear, "there's something important I want to ask you."

"I hope you're not looking for a loan. If so, you're barking up the wrong tree."

"You mean because dead hairstylists aren't at the top of the pay grade?"

"Dead hairstylists? I don't like the way you said that."

He shook his head. "Sorry. Tired. I meant hairstylists for the dead."

"Yeah, that sounds so much better," I said, laughing. "Okay, I admit stockbrokers probably make more than mortuary beauticians. Maybe I should be asking you for a loan."

He reached down and kissed my nose. "Anytime. Now get out of here." He gently pushed me away.

"Yes sir."

I stopped to pet Watson, who still hadn't quite found that special place he'd been searching for.

As I walked home, Adam's words about wanting to ask me something kept running through my mind. I thought about them all night—right up until the time I climbed into bed and fell asleep.

CHAPTER FIFTEEN

I woke up Friday morning to the sound of my alarm clock ringing. I reached over and hit the snooze button for another fifteen minutes of sleep. However, my mind was up and running even if my body wasn't. A strange dream had me tossing and turning all night. I was in a car race, driving Adam's car. Every other car around me looked exactly like his. I couldn't see all the drivers, but Betty Tuttwiler was definitely in the automobile next to mine. Clarence Diggs stood in front of our cars in his weird clothes, sporting his usual messy hair. His mouth was stretched in an awful grin, prominently displaying his missing teeth. He held up a flag painted with a clown's smiling face. Suddenly, he lowered his arm, signaling us to take off. I pressed my foot on the accelerator, but my car would barely move. It felt like it was trying to push its way through mud. I could see the finish line in front of me. Harold and Marvin, both in their clown makeup, stood there with their arms raised high above their heads. I kept pumping on my gas pedal, trying to get some momentum so I could finish the race, but the harder I pushed, the slower I went. Finally, I gave up and took my foot off the gas. When I did, my car took off and raced past all the other cars. I crossed the finish line and pressed hard on the brake. When I finally stopped, Harold ran up to my window and said, "Why, hello there, Hildee-dee-dee!" A wide smile was on his round, friendly face. "See, it was there all the time! All you had to do was let your car take you where you needed to go." Then he tipped his hat and he was gone—and so was Marvin. I was alone on the racetrack. The other cars had disappeared. I got out of Adam's red Saturn and stared up and down the track, trying to figure out where everyone had gone and why I'd entered the race in the first place. But the answer didn't come.

I lay in bed for a while, trying to figure out what the dream meant, but I couldn't make any sense of it. Finally, I turned off the alarm and got up. I'd started the coffeepot and had opened the cabinet to get some cereal when I remembered I was having breakfast at Gabe's. I took a quick shower, dressed, and downed two cups of coffee. Then I spent a few minutes with Sherlock. I felt guilty leaving him alone so much lately. He didn't seem upset. But then, how can you tell with a goldfish? A couple of minutes before nine, I said good-bye, and he wiggled his fin at me.

I could smell bacon frying when I walked past the downstairs kitchen. Mrs. Hudson stood at the stove. Minnie and Ida Mae sat at the table, laughing and carrying on like two old friends. Ida Mae saw me looking in and called out, "Why, good morning, Hilde! I hope we didn't wake you."

"No, you didn't," I said, smiling. "You all seem pretty chipper this morning."

Minnie reached over and patted Ida Mae's hand. "We're just friends enjoying each other's company." She turned her head so Ida Mae couldn't see her face and winked at me. I knew it meant she'd been working on her attitude.

"Good for you," I said. Although my comment sounded as if it was aimed at all three of them, Minnie knew it was specifically for her and she nodded. I said good-bye and pushed open the front door.

Several cars and a couple of trucks were already parked on the road near Ida Mae's house. I recognized Terry Nicholson's car and Albert Collins's black pickup truck. Butch's red pickup was next to them. Then there were a few unfamiliar vehicles. They probably belonged to the workers who were putting the roof on Ida Mae's house. As I walked across the road, a large truck carrying wood drove slowly past me and stopped in front of the boardinghouse. Two men jumped out and started pulling wood planks out of the bed. An SUV pulled up behind them, and three more men got out. These had to be the guys who were going to build our new garage. I could hardly wait.

I was almost to Gabe's house when his front door swung open. Adam stepped out on the front porch with Watson trotting merrily behind him. When he saw me, the little dog's rear end began wagging so vigorously I wondered how he stayed on his feet. I knelt down and opened my arms. He came running, jumped up on my lap, and licked my face like he hadn't seen me in years.

"How come you don't greet me this enthusiastically?" I said to Adam.

"If you really want me to lick your face, I'd be happy to do it," Adam said. "After you clean it off, that is."

"Now you sound like Gabe."

From behind us, I heard a car honk. When I turned around, I saw Billy driving over to where the other cars were parked. Adam and I waved.

"Nice of him to come and help again," I said. "He really is a good guy. Too bad he has Mindy to deal with."

Adam shrugged. "Sometimes men fall in love with high-maintenance women. I know how he feels. But what can we do? We're just gluttons for punishment."

"Ha-ha." I stuck my tongue out at him.

"Well, that's certainly ladylike."

"Who said I was a lady?" I asked, trying to look innocent.

"You don't have to. It's obvious."

I shielded my eyes from the sun, which was just starting to peek over the roof of Ida Mae's house. "You're being too nice to me. What are you up to?"

Adam grinned. "I'm just trying to get on your good side in case Gabe doesn't make enough waffles and I want yours."

"Oh, I see. There's a method to your madness."

The sound of a door slamming signaled that Billy had

gotten out of his car. I glanced over at him. "There's his highfalutin automobile. Doesn't look like much." I pointed toward the small row of cars lined up next to each other. "They all kind of look the same." There were actually several similar cars parked close together. From where we stood, it was almost impossible to tell the difference between them.

I started to remark about it to Adam, when the sounds of sirens split the air. I let go of Watson, stood up, and stared at the road. Two police cars raced up to the edge of Gabe's property and pulled into his dirt driveway, parking behind his old truck.

"What in the world. . ."

The officers in the first car got out and began walking briskly toward us. A man from the second car strolled a little more leisurely behind them. As he got closer, I recognized Detective Devereaux.

I swung around and looked at Adam, who hadn't moved from his spot. His eyes locked on mine. "Under no circumstances are you to call my parents, Hilde. Do you understand? I know we'll get this straightened out. I don't want to worry them."

All I could do was nod dumbly. Watson, sensing something was wrong, scurried back up on the porch. Adam opened the front door and let him in then closed it behind him.

"Mr. Sawyer, I'm going to have to ask you to stay where you are," Detective Devereaux called out.

The two police officers stopped next to me and waited for

the rather overweight detective to catch up. By the time he stepped up on the porch, he was huffing and puffing.

"What's going on?" I asked him. I could see that the men working on Ida Mae's house, along with the workmen who were building the new garage, had stopped what they were doing to watch the scene unfolding before them. Across the street, Ida Mae, Minnie, and Mrs. Hudson came out on the front porch.

"We're taking Mr. Sawyer into custody for the murder of Harold Tuttwiler," he said.

"Based on what evidence?" Gabe stepped outside on the porch and stood next to Adam. "Seems to me what you have is pretty flimsy. I take it you didn't even find Mr. Sawyer's fingerprints on the murder weapon."

Detective Devereaux didn't flinch. "No, but that doesn't prove he didn't do it. I would agree that what we had up to now was extremely flimsy," he said. "But all that's changed."

"And why is that?" Adam said.

"It would be better if we shared that with you downtown."

"I'd rather you told me now if you don't mind." Adam's calm demeanor seemed to shake the detective a bit. The police officers looked at him questioningly.

"All right, Mr. Sawyer. I'll tell you. And then these nice policemen are going to ask you to come with them. I'd really rather not handcuff you in front of your friends, so if you'll come along quietly, we can do without them."

"I won't cause any trouble," Adam said. "I just want to

know what it is you think you have on me."

Devereaux shrugged. "We got a call this morning from Clarence Diggs. He told us you phoned him last night and offered to pay him a substantial amount of money if he'd change his testimony about seeing your car at the cemetery. He also told us that you admitted killing Harold Tuttwiler."

Adam looked as shocked as I felt. "Detective, I assure you that I didn't make that call. Someone is obviously trying to frame me."

Devereaux smiled and shook his head. "Yeah, we never hear that."

I took a step toward him. I was so angry I felt a little faint. "You're wrong, you know. Adam had absolutely nothing to do with this. You're arresting the wrong man."

His eyes widened a little. "Miss Higgins," he said in a little softer tone, "I have no idea if this phone call really came from Mr. Sawyer. You have my word that I won't accept it as valid without checking it out thoroughly. But we have to take this seriously. We can't allow a possible murder suspect to flee. If we find there's nothing to it, we'll let him go. We're not the enemy, you know." He directed his attention back to Adam. "Do you have your cell phone with you, Mr. Sawyer?"

"It's in my pocket."

"Is it your only phone?"

Adam nodded.

"Please leave it where it is and come along with me."

Devereaux wore his authority like a badge. There was no room for discussion at this point.

Maybe he wasn't my enemy at that moment, but I sure didn't consider him a friend. Adam came down the steps and was led away by the police. I thought he'd say something to me or look my way, but he didn't.

Devereaux followed Adam and the officers to their car, where they placed Adam in the backseat. Then the detective turned around and gazed at me. I knew I had tears streaming down my face, but I didn't care. I was angry at the injustice of Adam's arrest and sad that a man with his character could be put through something so humiliating. Devereaux hesitated a moment and raised his hand as if saying good-bye. Then he climbed into his car and drove away.

For a few seconds, it seemed as if everything in Eden had stopped to take a breath. No one budged. Finally, a workman at Ida Mae's began to hammer again. As if it were some kind of wake-up call, the rest of us finally began to move.

Gabe walked down the steps and put his arms around me. I sobbed into his chest for a minute or two before he led me gently into the house.

Once we got upstairs, he guided me into his kitchen, where he handed me a couple of tissues. I wiped my face and blew my nose. "N–now what?" I said.

"Now we do exactly what we planned to do before this happened." His tone was steady and commanding, and I found that it calmed me.

"We're going to go talk to people? See if we can find out who really killed Harold?"

"Yes, but first you're going to have some breakfast."

"I can't eat anything, Gabe," I said, sniffing. "I'm not the least bit hungry."

"Hilde, you're not going anywhere unless you eat. I can't have you passing out on me."

"I'm not going to pass out." The truth was, I did feel a little light-headed.

"Sit."

I sat. Gabe poured me a cup of coffee then poured some batter into his waffle maker. I had to admit that as the waffles cooked, they smelled delicious.

By the time Gabe put a plate full of waffles in front of me, I was ravenous. Never being the kind of person who would eat to make herself feel better, it was a strange experience. Gabe prayed over our food, and I began shoveling his waffles in almost faster than I could swallow them. Gabe sat down across from me, but he only picked at his breakfast. Neither one of us said anything. I was thinking about the situation with Adam. Sticking food in my mouth became an almost automatic reaction.

"I wanted you to eat so you'd have some strength," Gabe said. "Now I'm afraid you'll faint from overeating."

"I've never heard of anyone passing out from eating too much."

"Me either," he said dryly. "But there's always a first time."

I jabbed the last bite of waffle on my plate. "I'm done," I said, chewing and swallowing as quickly as I could. "Now how are we going to save Adam?"

Gabe got up and got the coffeepot. He refilled both our cups. "Hilde, I want to ask you a question, and I don't want you to get angry with me."

"Right now I just feel numb. You won't make me mad. I promise."

He sat down and put both hands around his cup, staring at it instead of me. "Last night we talked about bribing Clarence Diggs. And today Adam is arrested for doing exactly that. Have you considered the coincidence at all?"

"The thought entered my brain for about one second. But I did what you told me to. I took it captive and pushed it out again. Adam didn't kill anyone. And he didn't call Clarence Diggs."

"You sound convinced of that."

"I am."

Gabe stared at me intently for a few moments. Then he smiled. "Good. We need to do some really good detective work, and I need you to be completely convinced of Adam's innocence."

"You don't have to worry about that." I cocked my head and studied his face. "Now you answer the same question. Did you wonder if Adam could have called Diggs and offered him money to lie?"

Gabe grunted. "No. Of course, the fact that his cell phone ran out of juice last night because he hadn't charged it in a while helped to convince me."

I sighed and shook my head. "So the only other phone available was yours. Have you charged it recently?"

"I cannot lie. I forgot."

"So last night you and Adam had two dead cell phones. What if I'd needed to call you?"

He made a snorting sound. "For crying out loud, Hilde. You could just walk across the street."

"You're giving me a headache, you know that?"

"I can't give you a headache, Hilde. I'm not quite that powerful."

I waved my hands around. "Okay, okay. I give. Now can we get back to Adam?"

"Sure."

"But will you promise me one thing?"

He frowned at me.

"Now that you've come out of hiding, will you get a regular phone? One that you don't have to charge? It would certainly make my life much easier."

He leaned back in his chair. "I'll consider it. At least I won't have to hear you gripe at me about plugging the stupid thing in."

"Thank you."

"You're welcome. Now if you're finished eating and telling me off, let's get going."

"And where are we headed first?"

Gabe thought for a moment. "I think we need to stick to the plan. Let's talk to this Albert Collins about the argument he overheard between Harold and Betty. See if we can get any other information. Then we'll go to the furniture store. Maybe if we can convince Harold's son that his father's argument with Marvin might have had something to do with the reason Harold was killed, he'll tell us what we need to know."

"That sounds good. But is there anything we can do to get Adam released right away?"

Gabe shook his head. "No, I don't think so. I doubt he'll be there long. When they realize he couldn't have made that call, they'll let him go. I don't think they have any other evidence strong enough to hold him."

"But won't they wonder if he used another phone?"

Gabe shrugged. "I don't know. It depends on what number was used to call Diggs. They'll try to track it. If it came from a phone that couldn't belong to Adam or me, that should clear him. If not, I'd be happy to turn my phone in to them. It won't take them long to figure out that Adam couldn't have used it."

"Do you think Diggs made up the call to clear himself?"

"It's possible, but improbable. My guess is that the murderer made the call as a way to implicate Adam. Diggs wouldn't know the difference. He doesn't know Adam's voice."

"Then we need to talk to. . ."

"Diggs."

I had to admit that seeing the creepy old groundskeeper again made me uncomfortable. But if it would help Adam, I'd do it. Then I thought of something. "But if Diggs tells the police we came to see him, won't that make it look like we're. . .what do you call it. . ."

"Interfering with an investigation?"

I nodded.

"If Adam really had called him, I wouldn't go within ten miles of the man. But he didn't, so I don't see how we could possibly be compromising anything."

I wasn't so sure about that, but with Gabe's background, I decided to trust him. Besides, I really didn't have any other choice.

We let Watson outside for a while. Then we put him back inside the house, where he curled up in a corner of Gabe's living room and went to sleep. We built a barricade at the top of the stairs so he wouldn't try to climb down into the store. Not because Gabe cared about any of the junk down there—but so Watson wouldn't tumble down the steps and hurt himself.

"You said Albert Collins is here?" Gabe asked when we got outside.

I pointed toward Ida Mae's house. "There he is. The guy in the blue cap."

Albert was pulling some large sheets of plywood out of

the back of his truck. As we approached him, he saw us and stopped.

"Hey, Hilde!" he called out.

"Hi, Albert."

"Adam okay? I saw what happened earlier." He took a handkerchief out of his pocket and wiped his chubby face. "This will all get cleared up. I know Adam didn't do anything wrong."

His expression was sincere, and I believed him. He'd spent his life running a popular Wichita restaurant with his wife. He'd sold it at a good price, and now he and Edie were retired. Anyway, they were supposed to be retired. Albert spent most of his time with Clowns for Christ and doing volunteer work at a large daily food program. God's Diner served hundreds of meals to low-income individuals and families in Wichita, and it had been the recipient of some of Albert's best recipes. Edie worked beside him, and she was also actively involved in her church's prison outreach. Although I hadn't known either one of them very long, I was confident of their veracity.

"Thanks," I said. "Albert, have you met my friend, Gabe Bashevis?"

"Sure," he said, sticking his hand out anyway. "We met the other day. How are you, Gabe?"

Gabe took his hand and shook it enthusiastically. "I'm good, Albert. Thanks for asking. Hate to keep you from your work, but we have a couple of questions for you if you don't mind."

Albert wiped his face again. It wasn't really warm outside, but hard work and extra padding were having an effect on the overweight man. Albert described both himself and Edie as "fluffy." Years of Albert's good cooking was the obvious culprit. "Anything I can do to help," he said.

I cleared my throat. "You told Adam that you overheard Harold and Betty arguing at last month's potluck dinner. What can you tell us about that conversation?"

Albert frowned. "You don't think Betty had anything to do with Harold's death, do you?"

"No, we don't think she did," Gabe said. "But we're looking for anything unusual that happened shortly before Harold was killed that might point to the reason someone wanted him dead. It's possible Betty and Harold's argument may hold some clues."

Albert nodded. "Well, hearing them argue certainly was unusual all right. They were a great couple. I've known them for years. Betty loved Harold."

"I'm sure you're right," I said. "Can you tell us what you overheard Betty say that night? Adam said there was something about Harold needing to tell the truth—and about a letter of some kind. Can you remember anything else?"

Albert stared down at the ground for a moment. "Let me see," he said slowly. "Seems like there was something else odd that Harold said. I'd kinda put this outta my mind. I don't like listening in on my friends' private troubles."

Gabe and I stood patiently, waiting for Albert to dredge up whatever memory he was attempting to unearth.

"Albert," Gabe said finally. "Betty said Harold mentioned that he was concerned about something illegal. Does that help any?"

Albert's eyes widened. "Well, for pity's sake," he said in a surprised voice. "When I told Adam about hearing them fight, all I remembered at the time was Betty's comment about Harold needing to tell the truth about something he got in the mail. But that's not what she said at all. She said he needed to tell the truth about some kind of blackmail." He shook his head. "Why didn't I remember that until now?"

Gabe reached over and patted the upset man on the shoulder. "Because you didn't associate your friends with a word like *blackmail*. Your mind changed it to something that made more sense."

"I–I'm sorry," Albert sputtered. "I hope I haven't caused Adam trouble over this."

"Not at all," I said, trying to sound reassuring. "Maybe this will be the break Adam needs to prove his innocence. Thanks, Albert."

"You're welcome. And if Adam needs anything, anything at all, you just call me, okay?"

We agreed and thanked him again for the information. As we walked back toward Gabe's place, I reached over and grabbed his arm.

"All Betty said to me was that Harold mentioned 'illegal

activity.' She didn't say anything about blackmail."

Gabe shook his head. "I wish we'd known before now that it was blackmail. It might have helped us."

"Should I call her, Gabe? Double-check this information?"

He thought for a moment. "When is Harold's funeral?"

"I don't know. Hold on a minute." I rummaged around in my purse, found my cell phone, and dialed Paula's number. After speaking to her for a couple of minutes, I hung up and put the phone back. Gabe had watched my attempts to find my phone in my messy bag with obvious amusement.

"You might want to clean that out someday," he said.

"Thank you for your suggestion," I said, not even attempting to keep the sarcastic tone out of my voice. "Now, to answer your question. Harold's service is tomorrow."

"Let's hold off calling Betty," he said. "I think we have what we need. I'd hate to bother her now. I'm sure she's trying to finalize arrangements and deal with family."

"Okay, but if we do need to contact her in order to help Adam. . ."

"Then we will," he said. "Now let's go see what Mr. Diggs is up to."

"Are we going to talk to Donnie?"

He nodded. "Let's do that after we finish with Diggs." He started walking toward his truck.

"Hold on a minute," I said. "You're not driving until you get your tags renewed. I'm not looking to get thrown into the cell next to Adam."

"They don't throw people in jail for expired tags, Hilde."

"The way things have been going, I'm not too sure. I'll drive."

We headed toward my car, which was parked in Mrs. Hudson's driveway. As we pulled out, Minnie, Mrs. Hudson, and Ida Mae were coming out of the house with pitchers of coffee and plates of doughnuts. They were all smiling and seemed happy to have a way to help out.

It took us a little over thirty minutes to get to Shady Rest. A quick drive through the cemetery led us to Clarence Diggs, who was on his knees weeding out a flower bed planted in the Garden of Peace, a section of plots located at the far back of the grounds. We parked on the road and got out. When he saw us coming, he stood up, not looking at all pleased to see us.

"What do you want?" he snarled. "If you're going to try to get me to change my story about your friend, it won't work."

Gabe held out his hand, but the old groundskeeper refused to take it. "We're not going to do that, Mr. Diggs," Gabe said, lowering his hand. "We're trying to get at the truth. We just want to know what happened."

Diggs cackled, showing his missing teeth. "Why would I want to talk to you about it? I ain't got no reason at all to help you and that killer."

"He's not a killer. . . ," I started to say. Gabe reached over and touched my arm.

"As I said, we just want to know the truth," he said to

the strange little man. "Can you tell me what you told the police?"

Gabe reached into his pocket and pulled out a one-hundred-dollar bill. In a flash, Diggs's expression completely changed.

"I—I guess that'd be okay. I mean, as long as you only want to know what I told the cops."

"That's it."

Diggs screwed up his face like he was thinking. I was certain he knew exactly what he'd said, and his act was for dramatic effect. "I told 'em that this Adam Sawyer guy called me. Told me he'd give me ten thousand bucks to change what I said about seein' his car."

"And of course, you told him no," Gabe said.

The old man's eyebrows shot up. "Well. . .I was going to."

"What does that mean?" I asked.

Diggs stared at the bill in Gabe's hand. "I—I hadn't made up my mind. But then he called back an hour later and said forget it."

"When did he call?" Gabe folded the bill in half, leaving it clutched in his fingers. Diggs's eyes were fastened on it.

"L–last night."

"And when did you call the police?"

Diggs swung his gaze back to Gabe's face. His face colored. "This morning."

"You were hoping he'd call back and give you another chance at that money, right?"

Diggs looked back and forth between us, obviously trying to decide just how truthful he should get. Finally, he shrugged. "Yeah, that's right. So what?"

"Mr. Diggs," I said as nicely as I could, "how do you know it was Adam Sawyer who called you? Did you recognize his voice?"

He shook his head. "Don't know what he sounds like. He said that's who it was."

Gabe blew out a quick breath in disgust. "And you just took the caller's word for it?"

The old man's face squinted in confusion. "Well, sure. Why would someone else offer me that much money? That don't make sense."

Gabe looked like he had an answer for him, but I thought it best he keep it to himself. "Did *Adam* say anything else?" I said before Gabe could get his mouth open.

Diggs thought for a moment. "Nah, that was it. Just that he'd pay me the money if I said I was wrong about the car."

"But you're certain the car you saw that day near the grave where they found Mr. Tuttwiler's body was a red Saturn?"

He looked at the money again. "I—I thought it was, but to be honest, all them cars look the same to me. I have a truck. Wouldn't drive nothin' else."

"Have you told the police that?" Gabe asked in a tight voice.

"Yeah. I told 'em. They know I'm not one hundred percent sure."

Gabe and I stared at each other. Sounded like the police had less proof than we'd realized. Gabe held the bill out toward Diggs, who snapped it up like a hungry fish after a worm. He flashed us his toothless grin and stuck the bill in his pocket. His green pants and red-checked shirt reminded me of Christmas, making the old man look like some filthy, disheveled elf. He dropped back down to his knees and went back to digging in the dirt.

Gabe turned and started toward my Cruiser. Guessing our interview was over, I followed him. I could see a line of cars parked up at the main office at the front of the cemetery. Except for my car, a large truck, and a couple of SUVs, they really did look similar. Except for. . .

I froze and stared at the various vehicles. Then I looked back at Clarence Diggs. Gabe, who realized I wasn't behind him, came back to where I stood with my mouth open.

"Goodness gracious, Hilde. You're white as a sheet. Are you feeling okay?"

I held up my hand, signaling him to wait a minute. Things I'd heard and seen over the last week began to drop into place—each one connecting to the other. Finally, they stopped.

"Wait here," I said to Gabe.

I ran back to where Diggs knelt on the grass and asked him a question. After scowling at me and telling me the answer wasn't any of my "durn business," I offered to take back the money Gabe had given him. He called me a "Miss

Smarty-Pants," but he confirmed my suspicions. I ran back to where Gabe stood, regarding me like someone who'd suddenly lost her mind.

"Gabe," I said breathlessly when I reached him. "I know who killed Harold and probably Marvin. Get in the car. We're going to the police station."

CHAPTER SIXTEEN

S o you actually solved two murders?" my mother said. "And you figured it out because this Diggs person said something about all cars looking alike to him?"

I nodded. "The way he dressed and something Betty Tuttwiler said about Diggs mixing up orders suddenly made sense. I knew Adam's car wasn't at the cemetery that morning. So I took out the impossible, and that left the truth."

"Clarence Diggs is color-blind. He only said it was Adam's car because of the shape. He was afraid to say he didn't know what color the car was. That was the reason he mixed up the orders at the furniture store, and he didn't want to lose another job."

Adam grinned at me. "Once Hilde realized that the car he saw didn't have to be red, the other things we'd heard finally came together. It was that red car that was keeping us from seeing the truth."

"That's right. You see, Billy Larkin's car looks a lot like Adam's, but it's green. So when Diggs saw Adam's car later that morning, he assumed it was the same one because of the design."

"Why did this Billy Larkin person kill your friends?" Mom asked.

"Although I figured out some of the story ahead of time," I said, cutting a piece of roast beef, "we didn't know everything until after Billy was questioned. Although he actually told us what happened in the car on the way to Marvin's graveside service. We just didn't realize it at the time. You see, as an insurance investigator, he had access to certain files. He'd heard that Harold's furniture store caught fire a few years ago. It was rebuilt and the inventory replaced. The insurance company paid on the policy, but one of their agents was convinced it was arson. Of course, it wasn't. An investigation declared it to be an accidental fire, but this man wouldn't leave it alone. Tried his best to keep Harold from getting his money. His reports went into the files that Billy read. He came up with a way to blackmail Harold. Threaten him with a civil lawsuit. Billy told Harold he had uncovered some evidence that would make him look guilty. If that happened, the insurance company could demand their money back. Something like that could bankrupt the furniture store, costing Harold's son his livelihood. Harold didn't want to take that chance, so he actually considered paying Billy off just to avoid trouble."

"You see, Billy needed money." Adam took up the explanation so I could chew. Thankfully, this was actual beef from the main part of the cow—not its cheek.

"Keeping up with Mindy's expensive taste was driving

him to bankruptcy," he said. "He thought he could shake Harold down for thirty thousand dollars. Not knowing what to do, Harold went to Marvin for advice, swearing him to secrecy. Marvin told him in no uncertain terms to turn Billy in to the police, or to at least contact his employer. In fact, Marvin threatened to take things into his own hands and turn Billy in himself. Unfortunately, Harold told all that to Billy. That's when Billy decided he had to get Marvin out of the way. He knew Marvin was going to be working on the electricity in the house that was being remodeled. He snuck in while Marvin was working. Marvin had turned off the breakers, but when Billy switched them back on, Marvin was electrocuted. It looked like an accident. Even Harold didn't suspect Billy. He never figured him for a murderer."

"Which was his mistake," I said, after swallowing. "He told Billy he wasn't going to play his game and that he planned to contact the authorities after he delivered Marvin's hat to the cemetery. Billy panicked. According to Billy, he drove there and tried to reason with Harold, even telling him to forget the money. When Harold wouldn't listen, he picked up a shovel and hit him. Then he tossed his body into the grave and drove away."

"He might have gotten away with it," Adam said. "Except that he made some rather major mistakes. He told Hilde that Marvin might not have been able to see the breaker switches because the box was under the stairs and it was dark. But supposedly, no one but Terry Nicholson had been in the house before Marvin went on the day he died. How could Billy possibly know where the breaker box was if he'd never been there? A call to Terry confirmed that he'd asked Billy to back Marvin up, but Billy had claimed he had to go out of town. Of course, he used the situation to do away with Marvin."

"He also tried to tell me that Marvin might have forgotten to turn off the breakers—that he'd been having problems with his memory," I said. "I should have suspected Billy right away after talking to Marvin's son Christian. If his father had really been having serious memory problems, Christian would have known about it."

Adam jumped in again. "He made another mistake on the way to Shady Rest for Marvin's interment. He claimed he'd never been there, but he mentioned that Maria Martinez had moved Marvin's resting place to a plot near a bench."

"How did he know there was a bench?" I asked, chewing. I was beginning to feel like one part of a two-member tag team. Amateur detective part *deux*.

"Don't talk with your mouth full," my mother reminded me gently.

"Also, he didn't want to drive his car to the cemetery," Adam chimed in. "Not because it was muddy as he claimed, but because he was afraid Diggs would see it and realize it wasn't my car he'd seen, but his."

"Did he know Diggs was color-blind?" Mom asked.

"No, not at first," I said. "But after I told him that Diggs had reported seeing a red car at the cemetery the morning Harold was killed, he suspected it."

"Although they didn't have all the information necessary to get me released and have Billy arrested for the murders," Adam said, "once Detective Devereaux picked him up and told him what he did have, Billy confessed to everything. Of course, when they matched his fingerprints to those found on the shovel, the jig was up, as they say."

"He admitted to calling Diggs, claiming to be Adam," I said.

"Actually, Billy was quite helpful," Adam continued. "Once he started talking, the police couldn't shut him up. He even explained why my name was written in Harold's scheduler."

"And why was that, Adam?" Mom asked.

"Harold told Billy that all the pressure he'd put him under had caused him to lose his temper with me for no reason. He planned to call and apologize to me the morning he was. . .killed."

Adam's voice broke with emotion. I was grateful he'd found out the truth, even if it did come from Billy. He knew his friend Harold had trusted him after all.

"He'd been edgy with other people, too," I said. "It must have been hard for him. He wanted to protect his son and his store, and even though Billy was trying to blackmail him, Harold didn't really want to get him in trouble. He still considered Billy his friend. In the end, his reluctance to call the police right away cost him his life."

"Betty knew someone was trying to blackmail her husband, but she assumed it was me." Adam reached for the bowl of potatoes and shoveled another helping onto his plate. Being released from jail seemed to have energized his appetite. I imagined he'd sleep pretty good tonight.

"Betty expressed her thanks to Adam and me at Harold's service," I said. "And she publically apologized to Adam."

"She didn't have to do that," Adam said through a mouthful of mashed potatoes. For a moment, I thought my mom was going to chastise him, too, for talking with food in his mouth, but she just smiled at him.

"So what happens now?" Mom asked.

I shrugged. "We go back to work and life goes on. Except things will be a little different in Eden. Now that Gabe is out of hiding. . ."

"Out of hiding?" my mother repeated with a slight note of hysteria. "What in the world was he hiding from?"

Adam and I grinned at each other. "That will have to wait for another time, Mom," I said. "One strange story at a time."

"Well, I certainly hope he's not dangerous."

"I can assure you, Gabe's perfectly safe," I said. "He intends to open up a real antiques store in Eden. Turns out he used to be a very successful dealer. He's got quite a stockpile of valuable antiques under lock and key in his basement."

My mother perked up at this news. She loves antiques and considers herself to be quite an expert. "I'd be happy to help him if he needs it," she said.

"I thought you said he was dangerous."

"Now, Hilde," she said, "don't twist my words. Antiques dealers aren't dangerous. My goodness."

Cue the *Twilight Zone* theme song.

"Ida Mae's roof will be finished next week," Adam said, spearing his last bite of roast beef. "We're also going to paint her house and help create a real bookstore, with a door that separates her living quarters from the store. And Mrs. Hudson's new garage should be done, too."

"I still say that living in that miniscule town is risky," Mom sniffed. She stood up and started collecting our plates.

"Can I help with the dishes?" Adam asked.

"No, you and Hilde go sit in the living room. I'm just going to rinse these and stick them in the dishwasher. I've got cake and coffee coming in a little while."

"Thanks, Mom," I said. "Everything was delicious. Thanks for having us over. I really appreciate it."

"Oh, for heaven's sake, Hilde," she said. "You make it sound as if I never ask you over for dinner." As the *Twilight Zone* music played again in my head, I decided not to point out that I could count the number of times I'd been to dinner at my mother's during the past several years on the fingers of one hand—and still have a few fingers left.

Adam and I strolled into the living room. Even though it was spring, the nights were still chilly. A fire burned and crackled in the fireplace.

Adam sat down on the couch and patted the seat next to him. I sank down and scooted close.

"So what do we do now for excitement?" I said, teasing him. "Life will seem boring without murders, tornadoes, or stints in the county jail."

Adam chuckled. "Thank you, but I'm looking forward to the mundane. It sounds absolutely wonderful."

"I feel like sleeping for about a week."

"Two weeks," he said. He leaned forward on the couch and turned his head to look at me. "But before these long naps we're planning, I have something to say. Something to ask you."

He had my attention. Suddenly, I didn't feel the least bit tired.

"Do you remember our first date?"

I nodded. "At Yen Ching."

"Yes. Do you remember the fortunes we got in our cookies?"

I laughed. "I have a photographic memory, remember? Yours said 'Prepare for an unexpected change. Your future holds many surprises.'"

Adam grinned. "Well, that certainly came true, but not quite the way I expected."

I patted his leg. "No one could have anticipated the things that have happened in the last several months. But we got through them together."

"Do you remember your fortune? The one you tried to hide from me?"

"You mean 'The love you've been waiting for is closer than you think?'" I smiled at him. "You don't actually believe fortune cookies have any real power, do you?"

He grinned. "No, but I'm sure God has a sense of humor."

"And what's so funny about my fortune?"

Adam shook his head. "Absolutely nothing. In fact, I want to give it back to you." He reached into his shirt pocket, pulled out a slip of paper, and handed it to me.

I took it and unfolded it. "'The love you've been waiting for is closer than you think.' You kept this thing all these months?"

He nodded. "You know, when we were kids, I thought you were the most wonderful person I'd ever met. Now, years later, I don't think that anymore. I know it." He got up, turned around, and got down on one knee. "Now for that question." He reached into his jeans pocket and took out a small black velvet box. He opened it to reveal the most beautiful diamond ring I'd ever seen. "Hildegard Bernadette Higgins, will you do me the honor of becoming my wife?"

I looked into his deep blue eyes and saw myself reflected there. And I knew I wanted to see myself in his eyes for the rest of my life.

"Yes, of course." My voice trembled even though I didn't feel like crying. I felt like dancing and praising God, shouting out the news of our engagement from the rooftops.

Adam slipped the ring on my finger and kissed me until my toes tingled. Then he stood up and held out his hand. "I think we should tell your mom, don't you?"

I nodded and let him pull me up. I was too happy to speak.

As I said before, life can be astonishing sometimes. The most wonderful things can happen when you least expect them.

As we walked toward the dining room hand in hand, I looked up and thanked God for being the kind of Father with whom everything is possible.

Even for a skinny girl with a weird name and a purple streak in her hair.

ABOUT THE AUTHOR

NANCY MEHL is the author of six novels, one of which, *For Whom the Wedding Bell Tolls*, won the 2009 American Christian Fiction Writers' Book of the Year Award in Mystery.

Nancy lives in Kansas with her husband, Norman; their son, Danny; and a puggle named Watson. She spends her extra time with her volunteer group, Wichita Homebound Outreach.

Nancy's Web site is www.nancymehl.com, and you can find her blog at www.nancymehl.blogspot.com. She loves to hear from her readers.